The Unforgotten Love

The
Unforgotten Love

A Story of Silent Love

Leo 1953

Copyright © 2024 by Leo 1953

All rights reserved. No part of this book may be reproduced or transmitted in any form or by any means, electronic or mechanical, including photocopying, recording, or by any information storage and retrieval system, without permission in writing from the publisher.

Disclaimer

The story depicted in this novel is based on true events. However, the author fictionalized certain aspects for creative purposes and to protect the privacy of individuals involved. The author acknowledges that the portrayal of characters and events may differ from actual experiences and perspectives.

ASIN: B0DK3MW91P

ISBN-13: 979-8343109368

Independently published on Amazon

www.amazon.com

Based on true events

Dedication

I dedicate this book to my wife on her birthday.

Without her support, this book would not have been possible.

Introduction

In the heart of Punjab, where the golden fields of wheat sway in the gentle breeze and the air resonates with the melodies of *bhangra*, a timeless tale of love and destiny unfolds. This is the story of Harsh and Naina, two souls whose lives intertwine amidst a tapestry of family, tradition, and the enduring power of human connection.

Their journey begins in the bustling city of Amritsar, where a chance encounter between their mothers rekindles a long-lost friendship, setting the stage for a series of shared experiences and heartwarming moments. As the children grow, their bond deepens, nurtured by shared birthdays, laughter-filled festivals, and stolen glances that speak volumes.

But fate, it seems, has other plans. Loss, relocation, and the complexities of life weave a tangled path, separating Harsh and Naina, leaving their love unspoken and their destinies uncertain. Years later, Harsh, now Harris, has built a new life in Canada, yet the memory of Naina continues to haunt him, a whisper from the past that refuses to fade.

Driven by a longing for answers and closure, he embarks on a journey that will unravel the secrets of the past and challenge the very foundation of his present. Along the way, he'll rediscover the strength of family ties, the resilience of the human spirit, and the enduring power of love that transcends time and distance.

Table of Contents

Chapter 1: The Journey to Forever 1

Chapter 2: Echoes of the Past 27

Chapter 3: Shadows and Silver Linings 47

Chapter 4: New Horizons and Lingering Shadows 75

Chapter 5: Dreams Rekindled in the Digital Age 93

Chapter 6: Roots and Wings: A Family's Growth in a New Land 113

Chapter 7: Cracks in the Foundation 127

Chapter 8: Rekindled Connections 143

Characters 167

Glossary 173

Leo 1953

Chapter 1: The Journey to Forever

1977

The Unforgotten Love

Section 1

All Aboard the Matrimonial Express

The rhythmic chugging of the train echoed through the Amritsar railway station, a symphony of anticipation and excitement. It was 1977, and the platform buzzed with a vibrant crowd of 55 people - family, friends, and neighbours - all gathered to embark on a 10-hour journey to Delhi for Harsh and Lavanya's wedding.

The booked railway coach resembled a vibrant tapestry of colours and personalities. Aunts and uncles jostled for space, their laughter echoing through the carriage. Children darted through the aisles, their gleeful shrieks adding to the festive atmosphere.

Harsh, his heart a blend of nervousness and exhilaration, helped his mother, Simran, onto the train. He assisted his mother in getting comfortably seated before he turned to greet his sister Vani, who held her lively one-year-old daughter Mona gurgling in her arms. His younger brother Sahil, ever the charmer, was already surrounded by a group of giggling cousins.

"Aman!" Harsh called out, spotting his closest friend amidst the crowd. Aman grinned, a playful glint in his eyes. "Ready for the big day, my friend?" he asked, clasping Harsh's shoulder. "Just remember, once you're married, no more late-night movie marathons!"

Harsh chuckled. "Don't worry, I'll find a way to sneak them in."

As the train pulled away from the station, the compartment transformed into a microcosm of celebration. The rhythmic clatter of the wheels provided a steady beat to the laughter, chatter, and occasional bursts of song. Children raced up and down the aisle while elders exchanged stories and blessings.

Harsh found himself drawn to a quieter corner of the coach, his thoughts drifting to Lavanya, his bride-to-be. He had only met her once, briefly during the initial introductions. Yet, her image lingered in his mind – her gentle smile, her intelligent eyes. He wondered if their arranged marriage would blossom into a love story.

"Lost in thought, brother?" Sahil's voice broke through his reverie.

"Just contemplating the journey ahead," Harsh replied, reassuringly smiling.

"Don't worry, *bhaiya*," Sahil said, his youthful optimism shining. "It's going to be a fantastic wedding. And Lavanya seems like a wonderful girl."

Harsh nodded, a flicker of hope igniting in his chest.

Vani, Harsh's younger sister, carefully settled her daughter Mona onto her lap, her eyes filled with joy and nostalgia. "Remember when we used to take this train to visit *Nani* in Delhi?" she reminisced, turning to Harsh.

"Of course," Harsh replied, a tender smile on his lips. "Those were simpler times, weren't they?"

Simran, their mother, overheard the conversation and said, "Indeed, they were. But life moves on, and now we're here, celebrating a new beginning for you, my son."

Harsh's aunt, a boisterous woman with a contagious laugh, gathered a group of ladies around her for a game of cards. "Come on, Simran," she urged. "A little fun will keep your mind off your worries."

Simran hesitated, glancing at Harsh. He gave her an encouraging nod. "Go ahead, *Biji*. Enjoy yourself."

As the night deepened, the train journey took on a magical quality. The gentle rocking motion lulled some to sleep while others engaged in hushed conversations, sharing their hopes and dreams for the young couple. Harsh found himself gazing out the window, the moonlit landscape blurring the past. He thought of Lavanya, imagining her anticipation mirroring his own.

As the train approached Delhi early the following day, excitement rippled through the compartment. Lavanya's family and Simran's brothers awaited their arrival at the station. The platform bustled with activity as porters unloaded luggage and families reunited after months of anticipation.

"Welcome to Delhi!" Lavanya's father, Mohin, greeted them warmly. "We're so happy to have you all here."

Simran's brothers, their faces beaming, ushered the guests towards a fleet of waiting cars. "Come, everyone," one of them announced. "We've arranged a comfortable rest house for you. Breakfast awaits!"

As the convoy of cars snaked through the Delhi streets, Harsh couldn't help but feel a sense of awe. The city's grandeur and energy were a stark contrast to the quiet familiarity of Amritsar. He was stepping into a new world, where he would soon embark on a new life with Lavanya.

The rest house, a spacious bungalow adorned with colourful decorations, provided a welcome respite after the long journey. The aroma of freshly brewed tea and sizzling *parathas* filled the air, tempting the weary travellers.

"Please, help yourselves," Rakshita, Lavanya's mother, urged, her smile as warm as the morning sun. "We want you to feel at home."

Harsh's stomach rumbled in response, and he gratefully accepted a plate piled high with delicious breakfast treats. As he ate, he observed the lively interactions around him. Lavanya's family moved gracefully among the guests, ensuring everyone was comfortable and well-fed.

Later that morning, as the guests settled in, some explored the city's iconic landmarks, while others opted for a restful afternoon at the rest house. Harsh, accompanied by Aman and

Sahil, decided to visit the majestic Red Fort, its imposing walls and intricate architecture, leaving them speechless.

As evening approached, the rest house became a vibrant celebration hub. Lavanya's family had arranged a lavish dinner, followed by an evening of *bhangra* and music. The rhythmic beats of the *dhol* drums filled the air, inviting everyone to join the dance floor. Harsh, caught up in the infectious energy, was twirling and laughing with his cousins and friends.

"This is amazing!" Aman exclaimed; his face flushed with excitement. "I've never seen you dance like this, Harsh!"

Harsh grinned. "I guess the wedding fever is contagious," he replied, eyes scanning the crowd for a glimpse of Lavanya.

As the night wore on, the celebrations reached a crescendo. The guests, their hearts brimming with joy, showered the couple with blessings and good wishes. Harsh, surrounded by the warmth and love of his family and friends, felt a profound sense of gratitude.

The first day in Delhi had been a whirlwind of emotions and experiences, leaving Harsh exhausted and exhilarated. As he finally retreated to his room, he couldn't help but think of Lavanya. He would finally see her tomorrow, and their journey together would begin.

The Unforgotten Love

Section 2

Sacred Rituals, Festive Rejoicing, and the Artistry of Mehandi

The Morning of New Beginnings

Harsh awoke with a flutter of excitement in his chest. It was the day of the *Shagun, Chunni,* and *Mehandi* ceremonies, a trifecta of celebrations marking the official commencement of his wedding festivities. As he freshened up, he couldn't help but reflect on the whirlwind of emotions he had experienced in the past 24 hours.

A knock on the door interrupted his thoughts. It was Lavanya's parents, Mohin and Rakshita, their faces beaming with warmth.

"Good morning, Harsh!" Rakshita greeted him cheerfully. "We just wanted to check in and see if everything is alright. Did you sleep well?"

"Yes, Aunty, thank you," Harsh replied, returning their smiles. "I'm feeling a bit nervous but mostly excited."

Mohin chuckled, "That's perfectly normal, son. Today is a big day, but remember, it's also joyous. We're all here to celebrate with you."

"Breakfast is ready," Rakshita announced. "We've arranged for a *'halwai,'* a special confectioner, to prepare some delicious treats for everyone."

Harsh's eyes lit up. "That sounds wonderful, Aunty. Thank you."

Soon, the rest of the house bustled with activity as guests gathered for breakfast. The aroma of freshly brewed *chai* and warm *parathas* filled the air, creating a comforting ambiance.

"Aman, try these *jalebis*," Harsh urged his friend, offering him a plate of syrupy sweets. "They're simply divine!"

Aman took a bite and nodded in agreement. "Wow, these are amazing! The *halwai* certainly knows his craft."

As they enjoyed their breakfast, Simran, Harsh's mother, couldn't help but express her gratitude to Rakshita.

"Thank you so much for everything, Rakshita," she said sincerely. "You and Mohin have been so welcoming and gracious."

Rakshita waved her hand dismissively. "It's our pleasure, Simran. We want this day to be perfect for Harsh and Lavanya."

Blessings and Bonds: The Shagun Ceremony

In the afternoon, the families gathered at a beautifully decorated banquet hall for the *Shagun* ceremony. A reverence filled the air as a *'pandit,'* a Hindu priest, commenced a small *'puja,'* a prayer ritual, invoking blessings for the couple.

Mohin performed the *'tilak'* ceremony as the bride's father. He applied a vermilion mark on Harsh's forehead, symbolizing good fortune and acceptance into the family. He then presented Harsh with gifts of cash and clothes, a gesture of goodwill and affection.

"Harsh, we welcome you into our family with open arms," Mohin declared, his voice thick with emotion. "May love and prosperity fill your life with Lavanya," Mohin declared, his voice thick with emotion.

Harsh bowed his head in gratitude, his heart brimming with humility and joy.

A Symbol of Love: The Chunni Ceremony

Following the *Shagun* ceremony, a group of women from Harsh's family, led by Simran, went to Lavanya's house for the *chunni* ceremony. They carried a vibrant red *'chunni,'* a traditional headscarf, sweets, gifts, and jewelry.

At Lavanya's home, excitement filled the atmosphere. Lavanya, adorned in a beautiful *lehenga*, awaited the arrival of Harsh's family.

As Simran draped the red *chunni* over Lavanya's head, a wave of emotion washed over her. She felt a sudden dizziness and swayed slightly.

Rakshita rushed to her side, concern etched on her face. "Simran, are you alright?"

Simran managed a weak smile. "I'm fine, just a bit dizzy. It must be the excitement and the long journey."

However, her condition didn't improve, and Rakshita insisted on calling a doctor.

The doctor arrived promptly and diagnosed Simran with low blood pressure, advising her to rest completely.

"Please don't worry about me," Simran assured everyone. "I'll be fine. The *chunni* ceremony must go on."

And so it did, with renewed warmth and concern for Simran. Lavanya's family showered her with love and attention, ensuring she was comfortable and well cared for.

A Night of Melodies, Merriment, and Mehandi: The Ladies Sangeet and Mehandi Ceremony

As the evening descended, the ladies of both families gathered at Lavanya's house for the *sangeet*, a night of music, dance, and celebration intertwined with the beautiful tradition of the *mehandi* ceremony.

The air resonated with the lively rhythms of traditional folk songs, and the women, young and old, joined in the joyous festivity. Laughter and cheerful banter filled the room as they danced the night away, their hearts brimming with happiness for the couple.

Simultaneously, skilled *mehandi* artists adorned Lavanya's and other women's hands and arms with intricate henna designs. The fragrance of the henna paste mingled with the sweet scent of jasmine flowers, creating an atmosphere of enchantment.

Lavanya, her hands outstretched, watched in awe as the artist created a masterpiece on her palms. "It's so beautiful," she whispered, her eyes sparkling with delight.

Aarna, her younger sister, teased her gently. "Don't forget to hide Harsh's name in the design! It's a fun tradition."

Lavanya blushed, a shy smile gracing her lips. "I'll try my best," she replied, her heart fluttering with anticipation.

Meanwhile, Harsh, surrounded by his loved ones, couldn't help but steal glances at the joyous scene unfolding in the other room. Their eyes met across the room, and a silent understanding passed between them. They were on the cusp of a new chapter, a journey they would embark on together, hand in hand.

With the *shagun* and *chunni* ceremonies complete, the *mehandi* designs drying on their hands, and the *sangeet* celebrations in full swing, the stage was set for the grand finale: the wedding itself.

The Unforgotten Love

Section 3

Golden Vows, Radiant Smiles, and Playful Traditions

The Haldi Ritual: A Golden Glow

The morning of the wedding, he dawned bright and clear, mirroring the joy that filled the air. After a hearty breakfast, Harsh surrounded himself with his family, laughter echoing through the room as they playfully smeared his face with a fragrant paste of turmeric, sandalwood, and rose water. The golden hue, a symbol of purity and prosperity, brought a radiant glow to his face.

"Careful, Vani!" Harsh playfully protested as his younger sister dabbed a generous paste on his cheek. "You're going to turn me into a walking turmeric statue!"

Vani giggled, "Nonsense, *bhaiya*! It will make you even more handsome for your bride."

Meanwhile, at Lavanya's home, a similar scene unfolded. Amidst the joyous chatter of friends and family, they lovingly adorned Lavanya with the same golden paste, making her skin shimmer with an ethereal beauty.

"Remember, Lavanya," Rakshita whispered as she applied the paste to her daughter's arms, "this is a time for new beginnings. May this *haldi* bring you happiness and blessings in your married life."

Lavanya's eyes welled up with tears of joy and gratitude. She nodded, her heart overflowing with love for her family.

The Regal Attire and Sacred Blessings

As the evening approached, the atmosphere crackled with anticipation. Harsh, dressed in a splendid Punjabi wedding attire, stood before the mirror, his reflection a vision of regal elegance.

His mother, Simran, couldn't contain her tears of joy. "You look so handsome, my son," she said, her voice trembling with emotion. Today, my long-cherished dream is coming true."

Harsh and his family then gathered for a '*puja*,' a prayer ritual seeking the blessings of their elders and ancestors. The air hummed with the chanting of sacred verses as the *pandit*, a Hindu priest, performed the rituals, invoking divine grace upon the couple.

After the *puja*, Amar, Vani's husband, he carefully helped Harsh with his turban and '*sehra*,' the veil covering his face until the sacred moment of unveiling.

"*Bhaiya*, you're going to make the most dashing groom," Sahil declared, beaming with pride.

Harsh grinned, his eyes twinkling with mischief. "Just ensure you don't trip over my *sehra* during the *baraat!*"

The Grand Entrance: Baraat and Excitement

The moment everyone had been waiting to arrive. The sound of drums and trumpets announced the arrival of the '*baraat*,' the groom's procession. Harsh, mounted on a majestic mare, traditionally known as the "*ghud chadi*," led the way. Vani and his cousin sisters playfully offered the mare lentils (*chana dal*), symboling prosperity and good luck.

The procession, a vibrant spectacle of music, colour, and jubilation, wound its way through the streets toward the exquisitely adorned banquet hall. As they approached, the excitement reached a fever pitch.

Amar, filled with joy, sprinkled '*Kewra*,' a fragrant floral water, from a silver sprinkler on the *baraat*, adding a touch of aromatic elegance to the procession.

Welcoming the Groom: A Union of Families

Lavanya's family eagerly awaited the arrival of the wedding procession at the banquet hall. At the entrance, Harsh's relatives made introductions to Lavanya's corresponding relatives. They embraced and welcomed each other, symbolizing the union of two families.

Jaimala: The Exchange of Garlands

The family then led Harsh and Lavanya to a beautifully decorated stage. The fragrance of red rose garlands filled the air as they exchanged floral garlands in the *'jaimala'* ceremony, a sign of their acceptance and desire to wed.

Harsh and Lavanya sat on the stage, their eyes locked, overlooking the joyous wedding celebrations. Wedding attendees from both sides revelled in the lip-smacking, delicious vegetarian dishes, their laughter and conversations adding to the festive ambiance.

Kanyadaan and Saat Phere: Sacred Vows under the Twilight Sky

As twilight painted the sky with hues of orange and purple, Harsh and Lavanya were seated before the sacred fire, surrounded by their loved ones. Mohin, Lavanya's father, performed the *'kanyadaan,'* the traditional maiden donation ceremony, while the priest chanted *'mantras,'* sacred verses.

The couple then stood up, their hands intertwined. They circled the sacred fire four times, their *'dupattas'* tied together in a knot, symbolizing their eternal bond. The bride followed the groom in the last *'phere,'* or circumambulation, after which she preceded him the first three times, signifying their commitment to support and lead each other.

With the completion of the '*saat phere,*' the marriage of two souls was considered complete. The air crackled with joy and blessings as the newlyweds sought the blessings of their elders.

Joota Chupai: A Playful Tradition

As the ceremony concluded, Aarna, Lavanya's sister, and her friend Zara seized the opportunity to engage in the playful tradition of '*joota chupai,*' or hiding the groom's shoes.

"Quick, Zara! Let's hide them where no one will find them," Aarna whispered excitedly.

Harsh's close friend, Aman, noticed and playfully intercepted their mischievous grins. "Hey, what are you two up to?"

Zara giggled, "It's a secret!"

Aman, ever the charmer, winked at Zara. "Well, I'm pretty good at finding secrets. And beautiful girls."

A playful chase ensued, filled with laughter and lighthearted banter. Amidst the shoe-hiding escapade, Aman and Zara were drawn to each other, igniting a spark of connection between them.

A Perfect Ending to a Perfect Day

The wedding celebrations continued as the night wore on, filled with music, dance, and heartfelt toasts. Harsh and Lavanya, now husband and wife, basked in the love and blessings showered upon them. The day had been a whirlwind of emotions, rituals, and traditions, but at its heart, it was a celebration of their love, a love that would guide them through the journey of a lifetime.

And amidst the joyous chaos, a new love story was quietly blossoming as Aman and Zara discovered a connection that would forever link their destinies to Harsh and Lavanya's special day.

Section 4

Farewell and Homecoming: A Journey of Love and New Beginnings

A New Day Dawns: The Morning After

The morning sun streamed through the curtains, casting a warm glow on Harsh and Lavanya as they awoke. Their hearts were still brimming with the joy of their wedding day. After a long and eventful night, they had retired to separate rooms for a few hours of rest, their minds still buzzing with the memories of the festivities.

As they gathered with their families and friends for breakfast on the banquet hall's open lawns, a gentle September breeze carried a hint of coolness, a refreshing contrast to the warmth of their love.

"Did you sleep well, Lavanya?" Simran inquired, her eyes filled with maternal affection.

"Yes, *Biji*," Lavanya replied, a shy smile gracing her lips. "It was a beautiful night."

Harsh, seated beside her, reached for her hand, his fingers intertwining with hers. "It was," he agreed, his gaze filled with adoration.

Vidaai: The Bittersweet Farewell

After a leisurely breakfast, the atmosphere shifted as Rakshita and Mohin began preparations for the '*vidaai*,' the emotional farewell ceremony. The bride, Lavanya, was about to leave her childhood home, family, and cherished memories behind.

Tears welled up in Rakshita's eyes as she embraced her daughter. "Take care of yourself, my darling," she whispered, her voice choked with emotion. "And remember, you'll always have a home here with us."

Mohin, his eyes glistening, held Lavanya close. "Be happy, my princess," he said, his voice gruff with love. "You've found a good man in Harsh."

Lavanya, her own eyes brimming with tears, nodded. She then turned to her family and friends, her hands filled with puffed rice. With a graceful motion, she tossed the rice over her shoulder, a symbolic gesture of gratitude and well wishes.

"Thank you for everything," she said, her voice thick with emotion. "I'll miss you all dearly."

Amidst tearful hugs and heartfelt goodbyes, Lavanya bid farewell to her loved ones at the banquet hall gate.

Aman, who had grown close to Zara during the wedding festivities, lingeringly hesitated to say goodbye.

"I'll miss you, Zara," he confessed, his voice soft.

Zara's eyes sparkled with a hint of sadness. "I'll miss you too, Aman. But we'll stay in touch, right?"

Aman nodded, a smile tugging at his lips. "Of course. We'll definitely stay in touch."

Doli: The Journey to a New Home

As Lavanya stepped into the beautifully decorated car, her heart ached with the bittersweetness of leaving her childhood home behind. But as she glanced at Harsh, a sense of peace washed over her. She was starting a new chapter filled with love and hope.

At the rest house, Harsh's family eagerly awaited their arrival. Simran, Vani, and Sahil had been busy preparing for Lavanya's homecoming, their hearts filled with warmth and anticipation.

As the car pulled up, a chorus of cheers erupted. Small children, their eyes wide with wonder, surrounded the newlyweds, eager to glimpse the bride. They touched her clothes and jewelry, their innocent curiosity a testament to the joy Lavanya's arrival had brought the family.

"Welcome, Lavanya," Simran said, embracing her new daughter-in-law. "We're so happy to have you."

Lavanya's eyes shone with gratitude. "Thank you, *Biji*," she replied, her voice warmed. "I'm so happy to be here."

Departure for Amritsar: A Festive Send-Off

In the afternoon, Harsh, Lavanya, and their entourage left for the Delhi railway station to catch the train back to Amritsar. Lavanya's parents and some close relatives were there to bid them a last farewell.

"Take care of our daughter, Harsh," Mohin said, his voice firm but filled with love.

Harsh nodded, his grip tightening on Lavanya's hand. "I promise, Papa. I will cherish her always."

The train journey continued the wedding celebrations. Lavanya's parents thoughtfully packed a feast of delicious food, fruits, and sweets for the *'baraat,'* ensuring the journey was as enjoyable as the destination.

The eight-hour trip flew by in a blur of laughter, conversations, and shared meals. Lavanya, surrounded by her new family, felt a sense of belonging she had never experienced before.

Homecoming: A Joyous Welcome

As the train pulled into Amritsar station, Harsh's family and friends were waiting, their faces alight with excitement. They greeted the newlyweds with a burst of music and dance, the rhythmic beats of the *'dhol'* setting the stage for a grand welcome.

The procession, led by Harsh and Lavanya, made its way through the streets of Amritsar, a vibrant display of *'bhangra,'* a traditional Punjabi folk dance. The energy was infectious, and even Lavanya tapped her feet to the beat.

Finally, they reached Harsh's home. Simran, standing at the entrance, welcomed them with open arms. She then performed a short *'puja,'* a prayer ritual, circling a water pitcher over Harsh's head.

"May this water cleanse away any negativity and bring blessings to your new life together," Simran said, her voice filled with love.

After each circle, Simran attempted to sip the water, but Harsh playfully stopped her, symbolizing his role as the house's protector. After the sixth round, Simran finally relented. Lavanya overturned a pot of rice with her right foot, signifying prosperity and abundance as she crossed the threshold into her new life.

A Love Story Begins

As Lavanya entered Harsh's life, a new chapter unfolded, filled with the promise of love, laughter, and shared dreams. The wedding celebrations had ended, but their journey together was beginning.

With their hearts intertwined and their families united, Harsh and Lavanya embarked on a path filled with hope and happiness, their love story etched forever in the tapestry of their lives.

Chapter 2: Echoes of the Past

1962

The Unforgotten Love

Section 1

School Days and a Serendipitous Reunion

In the bustling city of Amritsar in 1962, nine-year-old Harsh embarked on his academic journey in the 5th grade at a private middle school. His sister Vani, a year younger, and brother Sahil, a lively six-year-old, shared the same educational path. Every morning, the rhythmic jingle of a cycle rickshaw marked the start of their day. Vishwas, their father, a diligent government officer, had arranged for this humble mode of transport to ferry his children to and from school each day.

"Hurry up, you three!" Simran would call out, her voice laced with a mother's gentle urgency. "The rickshaw puller is waiting!"

The children would scramble, their laughter echoing through the single-story house built in 1952. They'd pile into the rickshaw, their school bags jostling against each other as they embarked on their daily adventure.

"Faster, Uncle, faster!" Sahil urged, his eyes sparkling with excitement.

The rickshaw puller, a kind-faced man with a gentle smile, chuckled. "Alright, little master, hold on tight!"

He pedalled with renewed vigour, the rickshaw gaining momentum as it navigated the bustling streets.

The children's school, a modest private institution, buzzed with activity. Eager young minds filled the classrooms with the sounds of their learning, their voices blending in a symphony of knowledge absorption.

The year 1962 brought an unexpected disruption to their routine. The war between India and China cast a long shadow, forcing the school to close its doors for two months. Harsh, Vani, and Sahil found themselves on an extended vacation, their days filled with a mix of anxiety and excitement.

In 1965, Harsh completed 8th grade and transitioned to a nearby boy's secondary school. Vani, now in 7th grade, was also ready for a new chapter, enrolling in a girl's secondary school within walking distance from their home.

The India-Pakistan war in 1965 closed schools in August and September, leaving Harsh and his siblings apprehensive and curious about the unfolding events.

On the day of Vani's admission, Simran accompanied her daughter, a sense of nostalgia washing over her as she filled out the application form. They waited patiently for their interview with the principal.

Simran's eyes widened in disbelief as they entered the principal's office. The principal, a woman with a warm smile and kind eyes, looked strikingly familiar.

"Bimal?" Simran gasped, her voice trembling with surprise.

The principal's face lit up with recognition. "Simran! Is that really you?"

The two women embraced, their laughter filling the room. It was a reunion years in the making, a chance encounter that rekindled a friendship forged in the halls of their college in Ferozepur.

"I can't believe it's you!" Bimal exclaimed, her eyes sparkling with joy. "After all these years!"

Simran, her heart overflowing with happiness, replied, "I know! It's been so long. Life has a funny way of bringing people back together."

Amidst the laughter and shared memories, Vani's admission was a mere formality. The school welcomed her with open arms, and the two friends exchanged addresses and phone numbers, promising to stay in touch.

As Simran walked home that day, warmth enveloped them. It was a day of new beginnings for Simran, who had rediscovered a cherished friendship from her past. Little did they know that this serendipitous encounter would weave a beautiful tapestry of connections, shaping the destinies of their families in ways they could never have imagined.

The Unforgotten Love

Section 2

A Knock at the Door: Reconnecting After Years

A knock at the door later that afternoon surprised Simran. To her utter delight, it was Bimal; her smile was as radiant as Simran remembered.

"Bimal! You didn't waste any time, did you?" Simran exclaimed, ushering her friend inside.

"I couldn't wait to catch up properly," Bimal replied, her eyes twinkling. "Besides, I had to meet the rest of your family!"

Harsh and Sahil, intrigued by the visitor, peeked shyly from behind their mother.

"Boys, come say hello," Simran encouraged. "This is Aunty Bimal, an old friend of mine."

Harsh and Sahil mumbled their greetings, their curiosity piqued by this unexpected guest.

"They've grown so much!" Bimal remarked, her gaze sweeping over the children. "And where's Vani?"

"She's still at school," Simran explained. "But you'll meet her soon enough. She's thrilled to have you as her principal!"

As they settled down for tea, Simran and Bimal eagerly shared stories about their lives since college.

"Vishwas has been a government officer for the last 16 years," Simran proudly stated. "We built this house back in 1952, and all three of our children were born here. It's been a lucky home for us."

Bimal nodded, her smile warm. "That's wonderful, Simran. Inder and I have two children as well – a four-year-old daughter named Naina and a two-year-old son named Laddi. Inder's a lawyer, working for a private company that manufactures woolen clothing."

The conversation turned to their past, reminiscing about their college days in Ferozepur.

"Do you remember that time we sneaked out to watch a movie?" Bimal giggled, a mischievous glint in her eyes.

Simran laughed. "How could I forget? We almost got caught by the warden!"

"You know," Bimal mused, "after we graduated, I moved to Rohtak with my parents. Then, after marrying Inder, we settled in Amritsar. I had no idea you were here too!"

Simran laughed. "It's a small world, isn't it? After college, I moved to Delhi with my family. We even built a house there. But then I married Vishwas, and his job brought us to Amritsar."

As the afternoon drew to a close, Bimal reluctantly said her goodbyes. "We'll come visit again this weekend," she promised. "With the whole family this time!"

A Weekend Visit: Families Unite

True to her word, Bimal arrived on a Lambretta scooter the following weekend with her husband, Inder, and their two children. Excitement charged the atmosphere as the two families met and mingled.

"It's a pleasure to meet you, Inder," Vishwas said, extending his hand in greeting.

"The pleasure is all mine," Inder replied warmly.

Meanwhile, the children wasted no time in making friends. Naina, with her infectious smile and boundless curiosity, quickly charmed everyone. She wasted no time making friends with Harsh, Vani, and Sahil, their shared laughter echoing through the house. Laddi, though a bit shy at first, soon joined in the fun, his giggles echoing through the house.

As the adults chatted and shared stories, the children played games and explored the neighbourhood, their newfound friendship blossoming under the warm Amritsar sun. It was a day filled with laughter, joy, and the promise of many more happy memories.

Naina's playful spirit captivated Harsh, drawing him towards her. He watched as she chased butterflies in the garden, her laughter like music to his ears. It was the beginning of a connection, a bond that would deepen over the years, unknowingly setting the stage for a love story that would transcend time and distance.

Section 3

From Childhood Companions to Budding Dreams: The Passage of Time

The initial meeting between Simran and Bimal sparked a beautiful tradition of frequent visits between the two families. Weekends became synonymous with laughter and shared meals as they alternated between Harsh's cozy single-story house and the second-floor house where Naina's family resided on rent. The children, Harsh, Vani, Sahil, Naina, and Laddi, formed an inseparable bond, their playful energy filling both homes with joy.

Festivals became even more unique, celebrated with grand feasts and shared traditions. During one such celebration, Harsh and Naina discovered a delightful coincidence – they shared the same birthday!

"No way!" Naina exclaimed, her eyes wide with surprise. "We were born on the same day?"

Harsh grinned, feeling a deep connection between them. "It seems like fate, doesn't it?"

The families rejoiced and decided to commemorate their birthdays together from then on, further solidifying their connection.

Simran and Bimal's college friendship blossomed into a deep familial bond. They spoke on the phone daily, sharing their joys, worries, and moments. Their connection became a bridge between their families, fostering a sense of closeness and belonging.

However, life brought its share of challenges. At the age of 45, doctors diagnosed Simran with diabetes.

"I'm going to have to make some changes," she confided in Bimal one day, her voice tinged with worry. "But I'm determined to manage it and stay healthy for my family."

Bimal offered her support, reminding Simran of her strength and resilience. "You'll get through this, Simran. We're all here for you."

Nurturing Talents and Shared Passions

As the years passed, Harsh and Naina grew, their focus shifting towards their studies and individual passions. Harsh, always drawn to music, started taking violin lessons from a local teacher. He also excelled at playing the *'Banjira Bulbul Tarang,'* an Indian banjo, often showcasing his talent at school music events.

"Harsh, your music is truly mesmerizing," Bimal complimented him one evening after an awe-inspiring performance. "You have a gift."

Inspired by Harsh's musical pursuits, Bimal encouraged Naina to learn the *'sitar,'* a beautiful stringed instrument.

"Naina, music is a wonderful way to express yourself," Bimal explained. "I think you'd enjoy learning the *sitar*. It's such a graceful and soulful instrument."

Naina, her eyes sparkling with curiosity, nodded eagerly. "I'd love to try it, Mummy!"

Harsh and Sahil, drawn by the allure of the television, which was still a novelty in those days, often cycled to Naina's house to watch Hindi movies and programs broadcast from Jalandhar and Lahore TV stations. Bimal, always a gracious host, would welcome them with warm smiles and delicious *'parathas'* cooked in *'desi ghee.'*

One evening, as they enjoyed a movie, Sahil exclaimed, "Bimal Aunty, your *parathas* are the best in the world!"

Bimal chuckled, ruffling his hair affectionately. "Thank you, Sahil. You're welcome anytime."

A Silent Promise: The Unspoken Understanding

Harsh's simple nature and kind heart left a lasting impression on Bimal. One day, during a casual conversation with Simran, she broached a delicate subject.

"Simran," Bimal began hesitantly, "I've been thinking... wouldn't it be wonderful if Harsh and Naina were to marry each other someday?"

Simran's eyes widened in surprise, but a smile slowly spread across her face. "It's a lovely thought, Bimal," she replied. "I'll discuss it with Vishwas."

After thoughtful consideration, Simran and Vishwas agreed. The prospect of uniting their families through their children filled them with joy. Ever the provider, Vishwas even added a second story to their home, a testament to their growing family and dreams. Meanwhile, Inder invested in a plot of land, envisioning a future home for his family.

"Bimal," Inder announced one evening, "I bought a plot today. We'll build our own house soon!"

Bimal's face beamed with happiness. "That's wonderful news, Inder! Our dream is finally coming true."

Dreams Take Flight: College Years and Unspoken Love

In 1970, Harsh completed his secondary education and joined a nearby boy's college, immersing himself in science subjects with the dream of becoming an engineer. Following her path, Naina enrolled in a girls secondary school, determined to pursue a career in law like her father. A dedicated student, Vani also began her college journey at a girls' college. Sahil, the youngest, was still navigating his secondary education.

During this period, Harsh and Naina's parents never openly discussed their intentions with them. However, their parents' frequent conversations and knowing glances hinted at something more. Harsh and Naina sensed an unspoken understanding, a secret pact that hovered in the air.

Yet, they never discussed it openly. The weight of their parents' expectations, coupled with the innocence of their youth, kept their feelings hidden. A silent love story blossomed in their hearts, unspoken yet deeply felt.

One evening, as Harsh was leaving Naina's house after a study session, he paused at the door.

"Naina," he began, his voice hesitant. I just wanted to say thank you for everything."

Naina's cheeks flushed. "You're welcome, Harsh," she replied softly. "It's always nice to study with you."

Their eyes met, and for a brief moment, a spark of something more flickered between them. But then, they both looked away, the unspoken words hanging heavy in the air.

Harsh and Naina's bond grew more assertive as the years went by. Their shared experiences and unspoken feelings weaved a tapestry of connection that transcended friendship. The seeds of love planted long ago continued flourishing, waiting for the perfect moment to blossom into a beautiful reality.

The Unforgotten Love

Section 4

College Days: Confidences and Unspoken Truths

Harsh's transition to college in 1970 marked a new chapter in his life. The science subjects intrigued him, fueling his dreams of becoming an engineer. But amidst the academic pursuits, he found solace and camaraderie in new friendships. One such friendship blossomed with Aman, a carefree spirit whose infectious laughter and unwavering loyalty made him a confidante.

One evening, as they sat on the steps of the college library, Harsh's heart felt heavy with a secret he couldn't keep any longer.

"Aman," he began, his voice barely above a whisper, "I need to tell you something."

Aman turned to him, his expression serious. "What's up, Harsh? You seem troubled."

Harsh took a deep breath. "My parents... they want me to marry Naina."

Aman's eyes widened in surprise. "Naina? Your childhood friend?"

"Yes," Harsh confirmed, a bittersweet smile gracing his lips. "We've known each other for years, and our families are very close."

"And how do you feel about it?" Aman asked gently.

Harsh's gaze drifted towards the distant horizon, his thoughts swirling with a mix of emotions. "I... I care for her deeply," he admitted, his voice barely audible. "She's kind, intelligent, beautiful... but we've never really talked about... you know, our feelings for each other."

Aman placed a reassuring hand on Harsh's shoulder. "I understand, buddy. It's a lot to process. But hey, if you have feelings for her, that's a good start, right?"

Harsh nodded slowly. "I guess so. But it's all so... predetermined. I don't even know if she feels the same way."

Aman's eyes twinkled with mischief. "Well, there's only one way to find out, isn't there?"

Harsh chuckled nervously. "I don't know, Aman. It's not that easy. What if she doesn't see me that way? What if it ruins our friendship?"

"You won't know unless you try," Aman encouraged him. "Just be honest with her, Harsh. Tell her how you feel. The worst that can happen is she says no, and you can both move on. But the best that can happen... well, that's a whole different story."

Harsh pondered his friend's words, and hope ignited his heart. Perhaps Aman was right. It may be time to leap of faith and express his feelings for Naina.

Meanwhile, Naina grappled with the unspoken truth that hung heavy in the air. She had overheard snippets of conversations between her parents, their cryptic remarks about her future leaving her with anticipation and trepidation.

One evening, as Naina and her mother, Bimal, were preparing dinner together, Naina decided to broach the subject. "Mummy," she began tentatively, "have you and Papa been talking about my future... marriage, perhaps?"

Bimal's hand paused mid-chop, a knowing smile playing on her lips. "What makes you ask, Naina?"

Naina fidgeted with her *dupatta*, her cheeks turning a delicate shade of pink. "I just... I've noticed how you and Papa sometimes talk in whispers, and you often mention my future..."

Bimal chuckled softly. "You're a very observant girl, Naina. It's true, we have been discussing your future. But don't worry, everything will unfold in its own time."

Naina's heart fluttered with a mix of anticipation and anxiety. She yearned to ask her mother about the possibility of marrying Harsh, but the words seemed to get stuck in her throat.

As the days turned into weeks and months, Harsh and Naina continued their separate journeys, occasionally crossing at family gatherings and shared celebrations. Each stolen glance, each shared laugh, and each unspoken word deepened their connection, a silent symphony of love waiting to be expressed.

Leo 1953

Chapter 3: Shadows and Silver Linings

1973

The Unforgotten Love

Section 1

New Beginnings Amidst Grief and Growth

1973 brought an unexpected and devastating turn of events for Harsh and his family. The sweltering heat of a May afternoon hung heavy in the air as a colleague of Vishwas's arrived at their doorstep, his face etched with worry.

"Simran *ji*," he began, his voice trembling. Vishwas *Saab* collapsed in the office. We're taking him to the hospital."

Simran's heart lurched, a wave of fear washing over her. "What happened?" she asked, her voice barely a whisper.

"We don't know yet," the colleague replied, his eyes filled with concern. "But we're doing everything we can."

Before Simran could process the news, the phone rang, its shrill tone piercing the silence. It was Lalit, Vishwas's boss.

"Simran *ji*," Lalit's voice was heavy with sorrow, "I'm so sorry to inform you that Vishwas is no more. We're bringing his body home."

The words struck Simran like a thunderbolt. Her knees buckled, and she collapsed onto the sofa, her world crumbling around her. Harsh, studying upstairs for his final graduation paper, rushed downstairs, alarmed by the commotion.

"*Biji*, what happened?" he asked, his voice filled with concern.

Simran looked up at him, her eyes brimming with tears. "Your father... he's gone, Harsh."

The news hit Harsh like a physical blow. He couldn't believe it. His father, who had left for work that morning in perfect health, was gone.

Hearing the news, Sahil burst into tears, his childish heart unable to comprehend the magnitude of the loss.

His face was pale, and Sahil took charge. His voice shook as he dialled the numbers of relatives and friends, informing them of the tragic news.

Within an hour, Vishwas's colleagues arrived, carrying his lifeless body. The house filled with the wails of grief as family and friends gathered to mourn the untimely passing of a beloved husband, father, and friend.

Coping with Grief and Preparing for the Last Rites

Vishwas's younger brother, Raman, and his family, who lived nearby in Amritsar, rushed to their side, offering comfort and support. Harsh, numb with shock, took charge, making arrangements for the funeral. With the help of a neighbour, he sent telegrams to relatives living far away, informing them of the tragic news.

They scheduled the cremation two days later, allowing relatives time to travel to Amritsar. Vishwas's elder and younger brothers and their families arrived the following afternoon, their presence a source of solace for the grieving family.

Simran's mother, sister, and three brothers arrived the following evening, their hearts heavy with sorrow. They embraced Simran, their tears mingling as they mourned the loss of their beloved Vishwas.

Lalit, a high-ranking government official and Vishwas's boss, took it upon himself to oversee the arrangements for the last rites. He understood the importance of honouring Vishwas's memory and ensuring a dignified farewell.

On the day of the cremation, mourners solemnly carried Vishwas's body to the cremation ground. Mourners, their faces etched with sadness, lined the streets of Amritsar. Vishwas had been a respected figure in the community, and thousands joined the procession to pay their respects.

Following Hindu customs and beliefs, they performed the final rites at the cremation. The priest, resonating with ancient prayers, guided the family through the rituals, offering comfort and solace.

As the flames consumed Vishwas's mortal remains, the priest announced that after a thirteen-day mourning period, they would gather at a nearby temple for the *'Rasam Pagri'* ceremony.

A Shared Vision: Introducing Naina

In the sad gathering following Vishwas's passing, Simran seized a moment of serenity to introduce Naina to her relatives and friends. She called Bimal, inviting her and Naina to their home.

"Everyone," she began, her voice a blend of sorrow and hope, "I'd like you to meet Naina. She is Bimal's daughter." There was a pause, and then she continued, "Vishwas and I had decided... we wanted Harsh and Naina to marry after they finish their studies."

A collective gasp filled the room. All eyes turned towards Naina, a shy 15-year-old standing gracefully beside her mother. Naina's cheeks flushed under the scrutiny, but her eyes held a quiet dignity.

"Naina's parents are also happy with this arrangement," Simran added, her voice gaining strength. "We believe they will make a wonderful couple."

A wave of murmurs and nods swept through the gathering. Naina's beauty and gentle demeanour had made a positive impression. Harsh, standing a little apart, felt a flutter in his chest. He had always admired Naina, but now, the prospect of their union felt exciting and daunting.

"They're perfect for each other," one of Harsh's aunts whispered to another. "Such a lovely girl."

Rasam Pagri: Passing the Torch

On the thirteenth day, amidst the sad gathering of extended family and friends, Vishwas's elder brother performed the 'rasam pagri,' tying a turban on Harsh's head. This poignant ritual symbolized the passing of the mantle of responsibility to the eldest surviving male member of the family, signifying Harsh's new role as the head of the household.

During the ceremony, Vikram, the charismatic leader of the employee's union, approached Lalit with a heartfelt suggestion.

"Lalit *Saab*," Vikram began, his voice filled with respect. I understand that Vishwas *ji*'s family is now without an earning member. Given Vishwas *ji*'s 24 years of dedicated service to the office, consider offering Harsh a job on compassionate grounds."

Lalit nodded thoughtfully. "It's a noble idea, Vikram. I'll certainly put forth this proposal at the next general meeting."

True to his word, Lalit presented the offer at the meeting, and the response was overwhelmingly positive. Everyone unanimously agreed to extend an employment offer to Harsh upon graduation, recognizing his father's contributions and the family's need for support.

The gesture brought a glimmer of hope to the grieving family. It reminded them that compassion and kindness can shine through even in the darkest times, offering light amidst the shadows of loss.

Harsh's New Path

Months later, after graduating, Harsh stepped into the role his father had left behind, joining the government office under Lalit's guidance. The familiar faces of his father's colleagues offered a comforting sense of continuity. Vikram, the union leader, extended a hot welcome.

"Welcome aboard, Harsh," Vikram boomed, his mustache twitching with a friendly smile. "Your father was a respected man here. We're glad to have you carry on his legacy."

Harsh, touched by the gesture, replied, "Thank you, Vikram Sir. I appreciate your support."

The office became a sanctuary for Harsh. The familiar routines and the echoes of his father's presence provided solace during a difficult time. Despite his youth, his colleagues treated him with respect and affection, often making him feel comfortable.

"Harsh, *beta*," Mrs. Kaur, a senior clerk, would say, offering him a cup of *chai*, "don't hesitate to ask if you need any help. We're all family here."

Harsh's dedication to his work soon became apparent. He approached his tasks with an honesty and diligence that mirrored his father's. Eager to grow and learn, he prepared for the departmental examinations. Within a year, he had cleared all the papers, his determination fueling his success.

Section 2

Dreams and Departures

A Helping Hand: Harsh Pursues Law

In 1974, Inder, Naina's father, extended a helping hand to Harsh, securing him a coveted seat in a three-year professional law course at the local university.

"Harsh, *beta*," Inder said one evening, his voice warm with paternal concern, "I know you wanted to pursue engineering, but this law program is an excellent opportunity. It will allow you to support your family and build a secure future."

Harsh's heart swelled with gratitude. "Thank you, Uncle," he replied, his voice filled with respect. "I appreciate your help more than words can express."

With renewed determination, Harsh embraced this new path. He juggled his studies with his job at the government office, and his unwavering commitment to his family was a constant source of motivation. He excelled in law courses, and his sharp mind and analytical skills proved valuable assets.

Vani, meanwhile, had blossomed into a bright and accomplished young woman. She graduated with distinction from a girls' college near Naina's house, and her academic achievements are a source of immense pride for her family.

"*Biji*, I did it!" Vani exclaimed, her face beaming joyfully as she showed Simran her graduation certificate.

Simran's eyes welled up with tears. "I'm so proud of you, my darling," she said, embracing her daughter tightly. "You've worked so hard, and you deserve every bit of this success."

Sahil, too, reached a milestone, completing his secondary education and enrolling in a boy's college. His youthful vitality and zest for life filled the house with laughter and energy.

Now, in her final year of secondary school, Naina eagerly anticipated her college journey. She dreamed of following in her father's footsteps and becoming a lawyer, her determination fueled by her passion for justice and equality.

Vani's Wedding: A Bittersweet Farewell

Meanwhile, Simran's focus shifted towards Vani's future. Simran yearned to see her happily settled; her daughter had blossomed into a bright and capable young woman.

"Raman," Simran said to her brother-in-law one day, "I think it's time we start looking for a suitable match for Vani."

Raman nodded in agreement. "You're right, *bhabhi*. Vani is a wonderful girl. We'll find her a good husband."

One of Simran's neighbours mentioned a young man named Amar, a bank manager with a promising career. When Raman and Harsh met Amar, his intelligence and respectful demeanour immediately impressed them.

"Amar seems like a fine young man," Raman remarked to Simran after the meeting. "He's well-educated and has a stable job. I think he would be a good match for Vani."

Simran agreed, her heart filled with hope for her daughter's happiness.

The wedding preparations started earnestly, and the household buzzed with activity and excitement. Although Vani was nervous about leaving behind the family, she was excited about starting a new chapter with Amar.

On the wedding day, the house was abuzz with guests and relatives. Vani, radiant in her bridal attire, looked like a princess. Simran, her eyes glistening with tears, embraced her daughter.

"Be happy, my darling," she whispered, her voice thick with emotion. "And remember, you'll always be my little girl."

Vani nodded, her own eyes brimming with tears. "I will, *Biji*. I love you."

After the wedding ceremony, Vani bid farewell to her family and friends, her heart heavy with sadness yet filled with hope for the future. She moved to Jalandhar with Amar, but the distance didn't diminish her love for her family.

Every weekend, she and Amar would make the 90 km journey back to Amritsar to visit Simran and the rest of the family.

"It's so good to have you back, *beta*," Simran would say, her face lighting up with joy as she welcomed Vani and Amar into their home.

Vani would smile, her eyes filled with love. "We missed you too, *Biji*."

Naina's Dreams and Harsh's Support

As Harsh delved into his law studies, Naina eagerly anticipated her graduation from secondary school. Inspired by her father, her dream of becoming a lawyer burned brightly within her.

"Papa," she asked, her eyes shining with determination, "when can I start preparing for the law entrance exams?"

Inder smiled proudly at his daughter. "Soon, Naina. Very soon. But first, focus on finishing your secondary education with flying colors."

Naina nodded, her resolve unwavering. She knew she could achieve her goals and make her family proud with hard work and dedication.

One evening, as Naina was studying at Harsh's house, she confided in him about her dreams. "I want to make a difference in the world, Harsh," she said, her eyes shining passionately. "I want to fight for justice and help those who can't help themselves."

Harsh looked at her with admiration. "I have no doubt that you will, Naina," he replied, his voice filled with sincerity. "You're one of the most intelligent and compassionate people I know."

Naina blushed, her heart fluttering at his words. "Thank you, Harsh," she said softly.

The Silent Promise

As they continued their conversation, a comfortable silence settled between them. They both knew, without having to say it aloud, that their connection was more profound than friendship. But the unspoken pact between their families, the weight of expectations, kept their feelings hidden.

For now, they cherished their time together, their shared dreams and aspirations weaving a tapestry of unspoken love. They knew their future was intertwined but also understood that they had to wait for the right moment to freely and openly allow their love to blossom.

The Unforgotten Love

Section 3

New Connections and Family Ties

Simran decided to rent out three rooms on the second floor of their house to supplement the family income. Baldev, a quiet and unassuming bachelor who worked in taxation department at a government office, became one of their tenants.

"Welcome, Baldev *ji*," Simran greeted him warmly as he moved in. "I hope you'll be comfortable here."

Baldev, a man of few words, nodded shyly. "Thank you, Simran *ji*. I appreciate your hospitality."

Baldev often dined at '*Maharaj Vegetarian Dhaba*,' a popular local eatery. Coincidentally, Baljit and Pushpa also frequented the same *dhaba*. They had recently moved to Amritsar from Ludhiana, seeking a suitable match for their elder daughter, Suman.

One evening, as Baljit and Pushpa were enjoying their meal at the *dhaba*, they noticed Baldev sitting at a nearby table.

"Pushpa," Baljit said one evening, "Baldev seems like a decent man. Perhaps we should consider him for Suman."

Intrigued, they conversed with Baldev, learning about his work and his quiet life as a tenant.

During their subsequent visits to Baldev, they met Sahil, Simran's youngest son. Sahil's youthful energy and cheerful disposition charmed them.

"He's such a lively boy," Pushpa remarked to Baljit one day. "And he seems to get along well with our younger daughter, Kumud."

Baljit nodded thoughtfully. "Perhaps we should consider him as a potential match for Kumud."

The threads of fate were weaving a beautiful tapestry, connecting these two families unexpectedly.

A Promise on the Horizon: Sahil and Kumud

Baldev and Suman's wedding in 1976 marked a new chapter, not just for the newlyweds but also for Sahil and Kumud. As the couple moved out of Simran's house, the space they left behind seemed to hum with the unspoken connection between the two young hearts.

Now a graduate, Sahil was drawn to Kumud's infectious laughter and how her eyes sparkled when they talked. He'd catch himself lingering at the *dhaba*, hoping to glimpse her.

The aroma of freshly brewed *chai* and the soft clinking of teacups filled the air as Sahil and Kumud sat on the balcony of Simran's house, their laughter echoing in the quiet evening. Baldev and Suman's departure left a bittersweet void, but it paved the way for their love story to blossom.

Now a confident young man with a steady job, Sahil reached for Kumud's hand, his heart pounding. "Kumud," he began, his voice husky with emotion, "I can't imagine my life without you. Will you wait for me?"

Kumud's cheeks flushed, a shy smile gracing her lips. "Of course, Sahil," she whispered, her eyes sparkling with love. "I'll wait for you forever."

Their fingers intertwined, a silent promise exchanged under the watchful gaze of the moonlit sky.

Meanwhile, downstairs, Baljit and Pushpa sat with Simran, their hearts brimming with hope for their children's future.

"Simran *ji*," Baljit began warmly, his voice filled with warmth. We've seen the love that Sahil and Kumud share. Having Sahil as our son-in-law would be an honour."

Simran's face lit up with a smile. "The feeling is mutual, Baljit *ji*. We adore Kumud, and we would be delighted to welcome her into our family."

Simran felt a wave of relief. Amidst her health challenges and the weight of responsibility, this blossoming love story offered hope.

"However," Simran continued, her voice tinged with a hint of concern, "Harsh is the eldest, and tradition dictates that he should marry first. We'll need to wait until he's ready."

Baljit nodded understandingly. "We respect your traditions, Simran *ji*. We're willing to wait until the time is right."

A wave of relief washed over Baljit and Pushpa. They exchanged grateful glances with Simran. The aroma of freshly brewed *chai* filled the air, a comforting scent amidst the delicate dance of tradition and young love.

They planned a '*Roka*' ceremony, a formal engagement, for the future. It was a promise that hung in the air, a testament to the enduring power of love and hope amidst life's uncertainties.

Section 4

A Mother's Worry, A Friend's Promise

Simran's once nimble fingers now fumbled with the buttons of her blouse, her vision blurring momentarily. The familiar sting of insulin prickled her skin as she administered her daily dose. Each passing day brought new challenges, her diabetes tightening its grip on her once vibrant life. Household chores, once a source of comfort, now felt like insurmountable mountains.

With a sigh, she reached for the phone, her heart heavy with a mother's worry. Bimal's cheerful voice on the other end brought a momentary respite.

"Bimal," Simran began, her voice betraying her anxiety, "We've decided to have a *'roka'* ceremony for Sahil and Kumud soon." She paused, the weight of her following words pressing down on her. "My health... it's not good. I'm worried about Harsh's future. Remember our promise?"

Simran knew a *'roka'* ceremony was a formal engagement in their Punjabi tradition, a step towards solidifying the bond between two families. And her promise with Bimal, a pact made years ago, now seemed distant and uncertain.

Bimal's voice softened. "Of course, I remember, Simran. I'm so sorry to hear about your health. I'll talk to Inder tonight and call you back."

Simran hung up the phone, her hand trembling slightly. The house's silence pressed in on her, amplifying the ticking of the old clock on the wall.

A Shattered Dream

Later that evening, the phone's ring startled Simran. She picked it up, her heart pounding with hope and dread.

"Simran?" Bimal's voice sounded hesitant. "I spoke to Inder... We're so happy for Sahil and Kumud, but... we won't be able to make it to the *roka*."

Simran's stomach churned. "Oh... I understand."

"And Simran..." Bimal's voice trailed off. "About Harsh and Naina... we need more time."

The words hung in the air, heavy and cold. Simran's grip on the phone tightened. "More time? How much more time, Bimal?"

"Naina wants to finish her law degree," Bimal explained, her voice laced with guilt. "It will be another four or five years."

Four or five years—an eternity, it seemed to Simran. Her vision blurred again, and tears stung her eyes. The dream she had nurtured for so long, the hope of seeing Harsh settled and happy, seemed to crumble before her.

"I understand," Simran managed to say, her voice a mere whisper.

She hung up the phone, her heart heavy with disappointment and a growing fear. The clock ticked on, its relentless rhythm a reminder of time slipping away, dreams deferred, and a mother's love that transcended all obstacles.

The Unforgotten Love

Section 5

A Mother's Plea: Seeking Solace in Delhi

Bimal's words hung heavy in the air, leaving Simran feeling lost and alone. Desperation gnawed at her, a mother's primal fear for her children's future fueling her resolve. With trembling hands, she reached for the phone, her fingers dialling the familiar number of her brother in Delhi.

"*Bhaiya*," she choked out, her voice thick with tears, "I need your help."

Her brother's steady and reassuring voice calmed her racing heart. "Simran, what's wrong? Tell me everything."

Simran poured out her worries, the broken promise, failing health, and the urgency to secure Harsh's future. Her brother listened patiently, offering words of comfort and support.

"Come to Delhi, Simran," he advised. "We'll discuss this together, as a family. We'll find a solution."

Simran packed her bags with renewed hope, her heart heavy but her determination unwavering. She embarked on the train journey to Delhi, the rhythmic sway of the carriage lulling her into a state of contemplation.

A Reunion and a Proposal

Upon arriving in Delhi, Simran and her mother, Laxmiya, made their way to Rakshita's house. Simran's connection with Rakshita ran deep, strengthened by their bond with Laxmiya's brother's wife. The familiar scent of jasmine flowers and freshly brewed *chai* greeted them as they entered.

"Simran!" Rakshita exclaimed, her face breaking into a warm smile. "It's so good to see you. And Laxmiya *ji*, welcome!"

The aroma of cardamom and freshly brewed tea greeted them as they entered Rakshita's home.

As they settled for tea, Simran broached the delicate subject that had brought her to Delhi. She explained the situation with Bimal and Naina in her thick, emotional voice.

"Rakshita," she said, her eyes pleading, "I'm in a difficult position. My health is failing, and I need to see Harsh settled before..." She trailed off, unable to finish the sentence.

Rakshita reached out and squeezed Simran's hand. "I understand, Simran. We'll do whatever we can to help."

Simran took a deep breath and continued, "Would you consider your daughter, Lavanya, for Harsh? I know it's a lot to ask, but..."

Rakshita's eyes widened in surprise. She glanced at her husband Mohin, who sat beside her, his expression thoughtful.

Mohin interrupted gently. "We need to discuss this as a family, Simran. But we appreciate your trust in us."

He turned to his wife. "Rakshita, why don't you call Lavanya?"

Lavanya, now a graceful young woman of 21, emerged from the kitchen with a tray of snacks.

Simran's heart ached as she looked at her, remembering the playful little girl with curly hair she had once known. She was beautiful, intelligent, and kind – everything Simran could have hoped for in a daughter-in-law.

"Lavanya," Simran began, her voice soft, "I know this is sudden, but would you consider marrying Harsh?"

Lavanya's cheeks flushed, and she glanced at her parents, seeking their guidance.

Mohin spoke up. "Lavanya, we've known Harsh's family for a long time. They're good people. And Harsh seems like a fine young man."

He paused and added, "But the decision is yours."

Lavanya looked at Simran, her eyes filled with compassion. She thought of Harsh, the kind and gentle boy she had met years ago. She knew that Simran was unwell and couldn't bear the thought of adding to her worries.

"I'll marry Harsh, Aunty," she said softly, her voice filled with resolve.

A wave of relief washed over Simran. She embraced Lavanya, tears of gratitude streaming down her face.

Before giving their final consent, Mohin insisted on meeting Harsh in Amritsar.

Simran nodded, her heart heavy with uncertainty. She had taken a leap of faith, but now, the waiting game began.

A few days later, Mohin travelled to Amritsar to meet Harsh. He returned with a positive impression of the young man, his dedication to his family and quiet strength resonating with him.

"He's a good man, Lavanya," Mohin told his daughter. "He'll make a wonderful husband."

Lavanya's heart fluttered with a mix of nervousness and anticipation. She had always admired Harsh from afar; his gentle nature and kind eyes left a lasting impression.

In March 1977, Harsh and Lavanya were formally engaged, and their families celebrated the joyous occasion. They set the wedding for September, a date that seemed both impossibly far away and tantalizingly close.

A New Path: Harsh's Decision

In July 1977, Harsh achieved a significant milestone: he completed his professional law degree. He now had the option to embark on a legal career that promised prestige and financial stability. However, his sense of duty and loyalty to his family prevailed.

"I can't leave my job at the government office," he explained to Simran one evening. "We need the income, and I want to honor Papa's legacy."

Simran's eyes filled with pride. "I understand, *beta*," she said, her voice thick with emotion. "You're a good son, Harsh. Just like your father."

As the summer progressed, the anticipation for the wedding grew. Despite the bittersweet circumstances, the families came together to celebrate the union of two souls, their hearts filled with hope for a brighter tomorrow.

Fate and circumstance intertwine their destinies, and Harsh and Lavanya are prepared to embark on a new chapter in their lives. Their love story is a testament to the enduring power of family and the resilience of the human spirit.

The Unforgotten Love

Leo 1953

Chapter 4: New Horizons and Lingering Shadows

1978

The Unforgotten Love

Section 1

Harsh's Golden Years

1978 dawned in Amritsar, painting a picture of contentment for Harsh. At 25, he had settled into his government job, and his dedication and integrity earned him the respect of his colleagues and the admiration of his boss, Lalit. The office, once haunted by the memory of his father, now buzzed with a different energy. Laughter echoed through the corridors, and the camaraderie among the staff felt like a warm embrace.

"Harsh, you remind me so much of your father," Vikram, the union leader, remarked one day, his voice thick with nostalgia. "He was a man of principle, just like you."

Harsh's heart swelled with pride. "Thank you, Vikram. I try my best to follow in his footsteps."

Despite the occasional loss, Harsh thrived in this environment. His colleagues, who had known him since childhood, showered him with affection and support. They shared stories of his father, their voices laced with fond memories, and Harsh basked in the warmth of their collective love.

The Arrival of Rajvir: A Celebration of New Life

In September 1978, Harsh and Lavanya's lives changed forever when they welcomed their first child, a beautiful baby boy named Rajvir.

"He's so beautiful," Lavanya whispered, cradling her son tightly. "Just like his father."

His heart is overflowing with love, and Harsh gently kisses his wife's forehead. "He's perfect," he murmurs, his voice thick with emotion.

The news spread like wildfire, igniting celebrations in Amritsar and Delhi.

Vani, beaming joyfully, arrived from Jalandhar with her two-year-old daughter, Mona, eager to meet her new nephew.

"Oh, he's so adorable!" Vani cooed, cradling Rajvir in her arms. "Congratulations, *bhaiya* and *bhabhi*!"

Lavanya, her eyes sparkling with maternal love, smiled. "Thank you, Vani. We're so happy to have him."

Mona, her eyes wide with curiosity, peered into the crib, her tiny fingers reaching out to touch Rajvir's soft cheek.

"He's so small!" she whispered, her voice filled with wonder.

Becoming an uncle filled Sahil, too, with joy. He tickled Rajvir's tiny feet, eliciting a gurgle of laughter from the baby.

"He's going to be a charmer, just like his uncle," Sahil declared, winking at Harsh.

Lavanya's parents, Mohin and Rakshita, arrived from Delhi, their faces radiating happiness. They showered their grandson with blessings and gifts, their hearts brimming with pride.

"He's perfect," Rakshita whispered, tears of joy glistening in her eyes. "A true blessing."

Even Aman, Harsh's close friend, couldn't contain his excitement.

"Congratulations, Harsh!" he boomed, clapping his friend on the back. "You're a father now! It's time to start saving for his college education!"

Harsh laughed, his heart overflowing with love for his newborn son. "I can't wait to watch him grow up," he said, his gaze fixed on Rajvir's peaceful face.

A Lingering Shadow

Amidst the jubilant celebrations, a shadow lingered in the background. Bimal and Inder, Naina's parents, were conspicuously absent. After Harsh's marriage to Lavanya, the rift remained unhealed, a silent reminder of the broken promise and the unfulfilled dreams.

Though grateful for the love and support of his family and friends, Harsh couldn't help but feel a pang of sadness in their absence. He missed Naina's infectious laughter, gentle spirit, and their unspoken connection.

Lavanya, sensing his melancholy, squeezed his hand reassuringly. "Don't worry, Harsh," she whispered. "We have each other, and we have Rajvir. That's all that matters."

Harsh nodded, his heart filled with gratitude for his wife's unwavering love and support. Their little family was his anchor, his source of strength in a world that sometimes felt uncertain.

As the celebrations continued, Harsh made a silent vow. He would cherish every moment with his loved ones, creating a happy and fulfilling life for his son Rajvir. And someday, the wounds of the past would heal, and the threads of destiny would once again bring Harsh and Naina together.

Simran, her health steadily declining, couldn't help but feel a pang of sadness. She had hoped that Naina would become a part of their family, but fate had taken a different turn.

"I wonder how Naina is doing," she mused one day, her gaze distant. She must be a beautiful young woman now."

A wave of regret washed over her. She had always cherished her friendship with Bimal, and losing that connection pained her deeply. But she understood Bimal's decision, her unwavering loyalty to her daughter.

As Harsh basked in the joy of fatherhood and the love of his family and friends, he couldn't help but wonder about Naina. He had heard whispers that she was excelling in her studies, her determination to become a lawyer as strong as ever. He longed to see her, talk to her, and bridge the gap between them.

But for now, he focused on the present, cherishing the precious moments with his wife and son, grateful for the love and happiness surrounding him, even as a longing lingered in his heart.

The Unforgotten Love

Section 2

A New Opportunity, A Heavy Heart

The year 1979 brought Harsh a bittersweet blend of professional growth and personal challenges. Surjit, the head of the Jalandhar office, recognized Harsh's legal acumen and offered him a position to manage the mounting court cases.

"Harsh," Surjit said, his voice firm yet encouraging, "I've reviewed your qualifications and experience. You're the perfect fit for this role. It's a demanding position, but I have full confidence in your abilities."

Harsh's heart swelled with a mixture of pride and apprehension. The opportunity was a testament to his hard work and dedication, but it also meant leaving the comfort of his familiar surroundings in Amritsar.

"Thank you, Sir," Harsh replied, his voice filled with gratitude. "I'll do my best to live up to your expectations."

With a heavy heart, Harsh accepted the offer. The daily commute between Amritsar and Jalandhar became his new reality, a constant reminder of his sacrifices for his family.

A Mother's Wish, A Brother's Vow

Simran's health continued to deteriorate, her once vibrant spirit now confined to a bedridden existence. The sight of his mother's frail form filled Harsh with a deep sense of helplessness.

One evening, as he sat by her bedside, Simran's weak but resolute voice broke the silence. "Harsh, *beta*," she began, her eyes filled with a mother's love. I want to see Sahil settled before it's too late."

Tears welled up in Harsh's eyes. He understood the urgency in his mother's plea. "Don't worry, *Biji*," he reassured her, gently squeezing her hand. "We'll arrange Sahil's marriage soon."

He turned to Sahil, who stood nearby, his expression a mix of sadness and determination. "Sahil, we need to talk to Kumud's parents. It's time."

Sahil nodded, his throat tight with emotion. "I'll do whatever it takes, *bhaiya*. I want *Biji* to be happy."

"Baljit *ji*," Simran said, her voice weak but firm. I want to see Sahil settled before it's too late."

Tears welled up in Baljit's eyes. "Of course, Simran *ji*. We'll arrange everything as soon as possible."

In July 1979, Sahil and Kumud were married in a simple yet heartfelt ceremony. Though unable to attend, Simran beamed joyfully as she watched the proceedings through video recoding.

Seeing her youngest son taking his vows brought a sense of peace to her weary heart.

Loss and Longing: Simran's Passing

A year later, in July 1980, Simran's battle with diabetes came to an end. Harsh, away in Jalandhar, received the devastating news with a sense of numbness. He rushed back to Amritsar, accompanied by his understanding boss, Surjit.

Mourners filled the house, their collective grief weighing heavily in the air. Vani and Amar had arrived from Jalandhar, their faces etched with sorrow. Harsh's heart ached as he saw his mother's lifeless form, her once vibrant spirit now at peace.

Naina's parents, Inder and Bimal, were conspicuously absent. Their decision to distance themselves from the family after Harsh's marriage had created a rift that seemed impossible.

New Life Amidst Sorrow

A few days after Simran's passing, Lavanya gave birth to their second son, Ashit. The arrival of a new life amidst the shadow of loss brought a bittersweet mix of emotions. Harsh, torn between grief and joy, held his newborn son, his heart filled with a profound sense of love and responsibility.

In January 1981, Harsh decided to return to the Amritsar office. His family needed him now more than ever, and he couldn't bear to be away from them any longer.

A Glimmer of Hope

Life gradually regained its rhythm. Sahil and Kumud welcomed two sons, Yoginder and Maninder, their laughter filling the house with joy.

Harsh's dedication to his work and family never wavered as the months passed. He found solace in his responsibilities and his love for his sons, Rajvir and Ashit, a constant source of joy.

But even as they embraced new experiences, the spectre of the past lingered. Harsh and Naina's unspoken love remained a silent ache, a reminder of a path not taken.

Section 3

Uprooted and Rebuilding

A Taste of the World: Singapore Sojourn

The year 1982 brought a welcome respite from the growing unrest in Punjab. Harsh, eager to create happy memories for his family, planned a trip to Singapore. The excitement was palpable as they boarded the plane, and the roar of the engines was a thrilling prelude to their first international adventure.

Singapore, a dazzling tapestry of modernity and tradition, captivated them. They marvelled at the towering skyscrapers, strolled through vibrant markets, and indulged in the diverse culinary delights.

"Papa, look at that!" Rajvir, now four years old, exclaimed, pointing at the majestic Merlion statue. "It's half lion, half fish!"

Harsh chuckled, scooping his son up in his arms. "It is, my little explorer. It's a symbol of Singapore."

Lavanya, her eyes sparkling with joy, watched her husband and son interact. The trip had been a much-needed escape, a chance to create happy memories amidst their challenges.

As Christmas and New Year approached, the city transformed into a festive wonderland. The streets shimmered with lights, and the air buzzed with the spirit of celebration. Harsh and Lavanya, surrounded by their loved ones, felt a sense of gratitude for the blessings in their lives.

Turmoil and Relocation: Leaving Amritsar Behind

The return to Amritsar was a stark contrast to the vibrant energy of Singapore. In 1984, the political unrest in Punjab had escalated, casting a pall of fear and uncertainty over the city. Harsh and Sahil, their families' safety paramount, decided to relocate to Delhi.

"It's not safe here anymore," Harsh explained to Lavanya one evening, his voice heavy with concern. "We need to leave, for the sake of our children."

Lavanya nodded, her heart aching at the thought of leaving their home and their memories, but she understood the necessity of their decision.

The sale of their ancestral home was a bittersweet moment, each room echoing with the ghosts of their past. Harsh and Sahil, their shoulders burdened with the weight of responsibility, packed their belongings, their hearts filled with sadness and hope.

In 1985, they bid farewell to Amritsar, their journey to Delhi marked by both loss and anticipation.

Building a New Life: Delhi Dreams

Upon arriving in Delhi, Harsh and Sahil's families found support and comfort in their relatives. Harsh's maternal uncles and Lavanya's parents welcomed them with open arms, helping them settle into their new surroundings.

"Don't worry about anything," Mohin reassured Harsh. "We're here for you. Delhi is your new home now."

Harsh's heart swelled with gratitude. "Thank you, Papa. Your kindness means the world to us."

The bustling metropolis of Delhi, with its chaotic energy and endless possibilities, presented a stark contrast to the quiet familiarity of Amritsar. Harsh and Sahil, their families in tow, navigated the challenges of adjusting to a new city, culture, and way of life.

"It's so different here," Lavanya remarked one evening as they sat on the balcony of their rented apartment, the city lights twinkling below.

Harsh reached for her hand, his touch reassuring. "It is," he agreed. "But we'll make it our own. We'll build a new home, a new life, together."

In 1987, Harsh's dream materialized as he built a two-story house in Delhi, symbolizing his resilience and determination.

Sahil, too, found stability in his new job at the Gurgaon branch of his bank, and his family thrived in their new home.

A New Chapter: Embracing the Law

Harsh's resignation from his government job had yet to be accepted, leaving him in limbo. However, once the authorities processed the official paperwork, he wasted no time enrolling in the High Court Bar Association in July 1987.

"It's never too late to chase your dreams," he told Lavanya, his eyes shining excitedly. "I'm finally going to become a lawyer."

Lavanya smiled, her heart filled with pride. "I know you'll be amazing, Harsh. You always achieve what you set your mind to."

In May 1988, Harsh further solidified his legal career by joining the Taxation Bar Association. Though he hadn't started practicing law, he already envisioned a new venture, a testament to his entrepreneurial spirit.

Amidst the challenges of relocation and new beginnings, Harsh and his family found strength in their bond, their love for each other a constant source of support. The loss of his mother and the distance from his childhood friend Aman left a void in his heart, but he refused to let it dampen his spirit.

As Harsh stood on the threshold of a new chapter in his life, he knew challenges and opportunities would fill the journey ahead. But with his family by his side and his dreams fueling his ambition, he was ready to embrace the future with open arms.

Lost Connections and New Beginnings

Amidst the whirlwind of change and relocation, Harsh lost touch with his dear friend, Aman. The distance and the demands of their new lives created a gap that seemed impossible to bridge. Harsh often reminisced about Aman and cherished the memories of their shared laughter and camaraderie.

As Harsh and Sahil settled into their new lives in Delhi and Gurgaon, they faced the challenges of adapting to a new environment and forging new connections. The absence of familiar faces and the lingering memories of their past in Amritsar created a longing and nostalgia.

Yet, amidst the challenges, they also found opportunities for growth and new beginnings. Harsh's legal expertise and Sahil's banking experience opened doors to exciting possibilities. As their families grew, their love for their children and commitment to providing them with a bright future became their guiding light.

The journey continued, filled with triumphs and setbacks, as Harsh and Sahil navigated the complexities of their new lives. The tapestry of their shared past and the enduring spirit of their families forever tied their hearts.

The Unforgotten Love

Leo 1953

Chapter 5: Dreams Rekindled in the Digital Age

1988

The Unforgotten Love

Section 1

A Technological Spark Ignites

The Terrace Conversations: Charting a New Course

The year 1988 found Harsh at a crossroads. At 35, he had a stable private job, a loving wife, Lavanya, and two bright sons, Rajvir and Ashit. Yet, a nagging sense of unfulfillment lingered. He yearned for something more, a career that aligned with his passions and challenged his intellect.

On warm summer evenings, Harsh and Lavanya would often escape to the terrace of their two-story Delhi home. The city lights twinkled below, a mesmerizing tapestry of dreams and aspirations.

"I feel like I'm stuck, Lavanya," Harsh confessed one night, his voice laced with frustration. "This job... it's not what I truly want."

Lavanya reached for his hand, her touch a silent reassurance. "I know, Harsh. But you're good at what you do. And it provides for our family."

Harsh sighed, his gaze fixed on the distant horizon. "I want to do something more meaningful, something that utilizes my skills and knowledge."

Lavanya's eyes sparkled with encouragement. "You will, Harsh. Just give it time. We'll figure it out together."

Their conversations often drifted toward their shared interests: music, movies, and the latest technological advancements. With a background in science and law, the emerging world of computers particularly fascinated Harsh.

The Allure of Desktop Publishing

One afternoon, while browsing a computer magazine, Harsh stumbled upon an article about Desktop Publishing (DTP). The concept of using computers to design and layout publications fascinated him. It perfectly blended his interests in technology, law, and creativity.

"Lavanya, you won't believe what I just read!" Harsh exclaimed, bursting into their living room, the magazine clutched in his hand.

Lavanya looked up from her book, a curious smile on her lips. "What is it, Harsh? You seem excited."

Harsh explained the concept of DTP, and his enthusiasm was contagious. "Imagine, Lavanya, being able to create professional-looking brochures, newsletters, and even books right from our own home! It's the future of publishing!"

Lavanya's eyes widened with interest. "That sounds incredible, Harsh! But do you think it's feasible? It must require a lot of investment."

Harsh nodded, his determination unwavering. "It does, but I'm willing to take the risk. I've found some institutes in Delhi that offer short-term DTP courses. I want to enroll in one and learn everything I can about it."

Embracing the Future

After careful consideration and discussions with Lavanya, Harsh enrolled in a reputable DTP course. The world of computers and design opened up before him, and he immersed himself in the learning process. His natural aptitude for technology and meticulous attention to detail made him a quick learner.

Within weeks, Harsh had mastered the intricacies of DTP software, his fingers dancing across the keyboard with newfound confidence. He experimented with layouts, fonts, and graphics, finding a new creative outlet.

"This is it, Lavanya," he declared one evening, his face excitedly glowing. "This is what I want to do. I want to start my own DTP business."

Lavanya beamed at him, her heart swelling with pride. "I knew you'd find your calling, Harsh. I'm so proud of you."

Securing the Dream: A Bank Loan and a Tech-Savvy Ally

Harsh's vision required a significant investment - a complete DTP setup, including a computer, software, and peripherals. He and Lavanya approached their bank for a loan, their hopes pinned on securing the necessary funds.

The young branch manager, Kaushik, listened intently as Harsh explained his business plan. His eyes lit up with recognition.

"Desktop Publishing?" he exclaimed. "That's a game-changing technology!" I've been reading about it myself."

Harsh and Lavanya exchanged hopeful glances. Kaushik's enthusiasm was a welcome sign.

"I'm impressed, Harsh," Kaushik continued. "But unfortunately, this project falls outside my lending authority. However, I'll gladly refer your application to the head office. I believe in your vision, and I'll do my best to advocate for you."

Harsh and Lavanya exchanged nervous glances. The fate of their dream now rested in the hands of strangers.

Days turned into weeks, and the wait seemed interminable. Finally, Kaushik called them with good news.

"Congratulations, Mr. and Mrs. Harsh!" he announced, his voice brimming with excitement. "The head office has approved your loan against your house property! Your proposal and your passion for this new technology impressed them."

Relief washed over Harsh and Lavanya. They had taken a leap of faith, and it had paid off. With the loan secured, they were ready to embark on their entrepreneurial journey, their hearts filled with hope and determination.

Harsh's life entered a new chapter, where he would combine his knowledge of law and his newfound passion for technology to create something unique and meaningful. The future was uncertain, but one thing was clear: Harsh was ready to embrace it with open arms, his spirit ignited by the possibilities ahead.

The Unforgotten Love

Section 2

A Leap of Faith

The Birth of a Publishing Venture

The year 1989 marked the realization of Harsh and Lavanya's shared dream. One of the rooms in their Delhi home transformed into a bustling publishing hub, filled with the rhythmic hum of computers, the scent of freshly printed paper, and the excited chatter of their two new employees, Subodh and Kushi.

"Subodh, make sure the layout for the annual issue is perfect," Harsh instructed, his voice firm yet encouraging. "This is our flagship publication, and we need to make a strong impression."

Subodh, a young and eager graphic designer, nodded enthusiastically. "Don't worry, Sir. I'll make sure it's flawless."

Kushi, their administrative assistant, bustled around the office, her cheerful demeanour brightening the space. "Tea, anyone?" she offered, her smile infectious.

Harsh and Lavanya's fortnightly magazine on indirect tax laws quickly gained traction in the legal community. The annual issue, released after the Union Budget announcement, became a highly anticipated publication, solidifying its presence in the publishing market.

The Winds of Change: Challenges and New Aspirations

By 1994, the landscape of the publishing industry had shifted dramatically. Fierce competition and rising costs made it increasingly difficult for Harsh and Lavanya to sustain their venture. The once-thriving business now faced an uncertain future.

"Harsh," Lavanya said one evening, her voice laced with concern, "we need to be realistic. The market is becoming saturated, and we're struggling to keep up."

Harsh sighed, his shoulders slumping. "I know, Lavanya. But I've poured my heart and soul into this business. It's hard to let go."

Lavanya reached out and took his hand, her touch reassuring. "I understand. But we also need to think about the boys. Rajvir and Ashit will need further education soon. Perhaps it's time to explore new opportunities."

Harsh nodded slowly, his mind racing with possibilities. For some time, the idea of moving abroad and providing his sons with a world-class education lingered in his thoughts. Canada's reputation for welcoming immigrants and robust education system made it an attractive option.

A Bold Decision: The Canadian Dream

After careful consideration and countless discussions, Harsh and Lavanya made a bold decision. They would apply for Canadian immigration, leveraging Harsh's experience as a magazine editor.

"It's a big step, Lavanya," Harsh said, his voice filled with excitement and trepidation. "But I believe it's the right one for our family's future."

Lavanya nodded, her eyes shining with determination. "I trust you, Harsh. Let's do this."

When their application for permanent residence was approved in March 1995, they felt a wave of relief wash over them. They wound up their publishing business with mixed emotions, sold their beloved Delhi home, and repaid the bank loan.

In July 1995, Harsh, Lavanya, Rajvir, and Ashit embarked on a new adventure, their lives packed into six suitcases. As they boarded the plane to Toronto, a sense of loss and anticipation filled their hearts. They were leaving behind their familiar world, extended family, and the comforts of home. But they were also stepping into a future filled with possibilities where their dreams could take flight.

A New World: Challenges and Resilience

The initial euphoria of their arrival soon gave way to the harsh realities of starting anew in a foreign land. The language barrier, the cultural differences, and the struggle to find employment tested their resilience.

"I never thought it would be this hard," Lavanya confessed to Harsh one evening, her voice thick with frustration. "We've been here for months, and we still haven't found jobs."

Harsh, though equally disheartened, tried to remain optimistic. "We'll get through this, Lavanya. We have each other, and we have our skills. We just need to keep trying."

They signed up with employment agencies, scoured newspapers for job listings, and spent hours at the library, using the computers to search for opportunities online. Their computer skills, honed during their publishing venture, proved to be a valuable asset.

"At least we know how to use these machines," Harsh remarked wryly. "That's got to count for something."

Despite their efforts, the need for Canadian experience and education proved challenging. Rejection letters piled up, each one a blow to their confidence. But they refused to give up. They had come too far and sacrificed too much to let their dreams slip away.

As they navigated the challenges of their new life, Harsh and Lavanya clung to each other, their love a beacon of hope in the face of adversity. They knew that with perseverance and determination, they would eventually find their footing in this new land, their dreams rekindled, and their spirits soaring.

The Unforgotten Love

Section 3

Adaptation, Expansion, and a Lingering Longing

Finding a Foothold: New Jobs and New Routines

The rhythmic whir of the conveyor belt, the scent of freshly laundered fabrics, and the chatter of coworkers in various languages filled the air as Lavanya, Rajvir, and Ashit began their shifts at the used clothing sorting facility. It was far from their aspirations, but honest work was a stepping stone towards a better future.

"Remember," Lavanya reminded her sons, her voice firm yet encouraging, "every experience is a learning opportunity. We'll find our way."

Rajvir and Ashit, though initially hesitant, embraced their new roles, balancing work with their studies. The school hallways buzzed with a unique energy, a blend of diverse cultures and languages, but the boys navigated it with resilience, their thirst for knowledge undiminished.

Meanwhile, Harsh found himself amidst the rhythmic clanking of machinery on the factory floor, his hands deftly assembling auto parts. The physical labour was demanding, but his mind remained sharp, focused on becoming a licensed immigration consultant.

"It's not easy," he confided in Lavanya one evening, the weariness evident in his voice, "but it's temporary. I'll make it work."

Lavanya, her hand resting on his shoulder, offered a reassuring smile. "I know you will, Harsh. You always do."

A New Identity: Harris Takes Flight

In the summer of 1997, Harsh made a symbolic gesture of embracing his new life in Canada.

"From now on," he declared to his family one evening, his voice tinged with nervousness, "I will be called Harris."

Lavanya smiled, taking his hand. "It suits you," she whispered. "A fresh start, a new name."

Rajvir and Ashit, ever adaptable, quickly adopted the new name, their young voices echoing "Harris" with a playful lilt.

Harris's perseverance paid off. He passed his licensing exams and became a Regulated Canadian Immigration Consultant. The news filled him with a sense of accomplishment he hadn't felt in years.

"I did it, Lavanya!" he exclaimed, embracing her joyfully. "We're finally on the right track!"

With his newly acquired license, Harris launched his immigration consultancy. The familiar world of laws and regulations and his passion for helping others ignited a renewed sense of purpose. He thrived in his new role, and his expertise and genuine empathy drew clients to him.

The years flew by, marked by hard work, sacrifice, and the quiet satisfaction of building a new life.

In 1998, they achieved a significant milestone—they bought their first condo.

"We did it!" Harris exclaimed, swinging Lavanya around in their new living room.

A Family Grows: Rajvir's Wedding

Time flew by, marked by the milestones of their new life in Canada. Rajvir, now a confident young man, graduated with a degree in finance and secured a promising job at a bank.

"We're so proud of you, Rajvir," Harris beamed, his chest swelling with paternal pride.

In February 1999, Rajvir married Geetanjali, a beautiful young woman from Delhi. The wedding, a vibrant fusion of Indian and Canadian traditions, brought the family together in celebration.

Lavanya, her eyes sparkling with joy, watched as her son and his bride exchanged vows. "They're perfect for each other," she whispered to Harris, her voice filled with emotion.

Harris nodded, a bittersweet smile playing on his lips. He couldn't help but think of Naina, the girl he had left behind in Amritsar.

The Ghost of Naina

Despite the outward signs of progress, some of Harris remained tethered to the past. With every step forward, he felt himself moving further away from Naina.

As the city slept late at night, memories of Naina would flood his mind – her laughter, gentle touch, the unspoken promise that once bound them. He couldn't shake the feeling that he had left a part of himself behind in Amritsar.

The memory of Simran's tearful phone call, Bimal's hesitant explanation, and the following crushing disappointment haunted him. He longed to see Naina again, understand the reasons behind their separation, and find closure.

"Why did they change their minds?" he'd often wonder, the question echoing in the silence of his thoughts. "What happened after Sahil's engagement? Did Naina ever feel the same way about me?"

Unanswered questions gnawed at him, constantly reminding him of the love he had lost. He longed to see Naina, understand what had transpired, and find closure. But the distance and the years that had passed seemed insurmountable.

One evening, a wave of longing washed over him as he gazed at the Toronto skyline.

"Naina," he whispered, his voice heavy with emotion, "I never stopped thinking about you. I never stopped loving you."

The city lights twinkled in the distance, their cold glow contrasting starkly with the warmth of his memories. Harris knew that he had to move on, to embrace the life he had built with Lavanya and his sons. But a part of his heart would always belong to Naina, a love that had blossomed in the tapestry of their shared childhood and would forever remain etched in his memory.

The Unforgotten Love

Leo 1953

Chapter 6: Roots and Wings: A Family's Growth in a New Land

2000

The Unforgotten Love

Section 1

New Citizens, New Beginnings

Embracing a New Identity

The crisp, parchment-like feel of the citizenship certificate sent a shiver of excitement through Harris. It was July 2000, and after five years of calling Canada home, he, Lavanya, Rajvir, and Ashit had officially become Canadian citizens.

"We're Canadians now!" Rajvir exclaimed, his voice echoing in the quiet government office.

Ashit, ever the pragmatist, added, "That means we can finally get Canadian passports!"

Lavanya, her eyes glistening with pride, reached for Harris's hand. "We've come a long way, haven't we?"

Harris nodded, a warmth spreading through his chest. "We have, Lavanya. We've built a good life here."

The maple leaf flag, hanging proudly in their living room, seemed to flutter in agreement. Its vibrant colours symbolized the opportunities and freedoms they had found in their adopted homeland.

Expanding Horizons

Life in Toronto continued its steady rhythm. Geetanjali, Rajvir's wife, joined the workforce, and her IT skills secured her a position at the head office of a local bank. The familiar sounds of keyboard clicks and the soft glow of the computer screen filled their evenings, a reminder of the publishing venture that had brought them to Canada.

In February 2003, the pitter-patter of tiny feet announced the arrival of Saarah, Rajvir and Geetanjali's first child. The house overflowed with the sweet scent of baby powder and the gentle lullaby of Lavanya's voice as she rocked her granddaughter to sleep.

"She's so beautiful," Lavanya cooed, her heart melting at Saarah's tiny fingers curling around hers.

Harris, peering over her shoulder, couldn't help but agree. "She's perfect," he whispered, a sense of wonder filling his chest.

New Love, New Dreams

Ashit, meanwhile, was nearing the end of his accountancy studies at the university. Amidst the textbooks and exams, he had found love with Divya, a vibrant young woman from Delhi who worked at a call center in Toronto. Their shared cultural background and dreams for the future drew them together, their love story blossoming amidst the city's vibrant energy.

"I can't imagine my life without her, Mom," Ashit confided in Lavanya one evening, his face glowing with happiness. "She's the one."

Lavanya smiled, her heart warmed by her son's newfound love. "I'm so happy for you, *beta*," she said, squeezing his hand. "She seems like a wonderful girl."

In November 2003, Ashit and Divya were married, and their wedding was a joyous celebration of love and cultural heritage. The rhythmic beats of the *dhol* and the vibrant colours of traditional attire filled the banquet hall, creating an atmosphere of pure joy.

"I can't believe we're finally married!" Divya exclaimed, her laughter ringing through the banquet hall.

Ashit, his eyes locked with hers, couldn't contain his smile. "Me neither. I'm the luckiest man in the world."

Spreading Wings: Rajvir's New Home

As the family expanded, Rajvir and Geetanjali created their own space. They purchased a cozy house in Toronto, their hearts filled with excitement and a touch of trepidation.

"It's a big step," Rajvir admitted to his parents, his voice laced with nervousness and anticipation. "But we're ready."

Although sad to see their son and his family move out, Harris and Lavanya were proud of their independence and determination.

"You've grown into a fine young man, Rajvir," Harris said, his voice filled with paternal pride. "We're so proud of you."

"We'll miss you, *beta*," Lavanya said, her voice thick with emotion as she hugged Rajvir goodbye.

Rajvir, his own eyes glistening with tears, reassured her. "We'll be just a phone call away, Mummy. And you're always welcome to visit."

A New Assignment, A New Home

Ashit's graduation in 2004 marked another milestone. He secured a position at a bank, and his dedication and hard work earned him a promotion to head their Hong Kong office. It was a bittersweet opportunity, a chance to further his career, and a journey that would take him far from his family.

In February 2005, Ashit and Divya relocated to Hong Kong with their young son, Tanveer, born in October 2004. The farewells were tearful, and the distance was heavy on their hearts.

"We'll miss you terribly," Lavanya sobbed, clinging to Ashit.

Ashit, thick with emotion, promised, "We'll be back to visit as often as we can, Mummy. And we'll call every week."

Grandparents' Bliss: Tania's Arrival

In Toronto, Harris and Lavanya's joy multiplied in November 2005 with the birth of Rajvir and Geetanjali's second daughter, Tania. The family, now spread across continents, remained connected through phone calls, letters, and the occasional visit.

Harris and Lavanya, now grandparents of three beautiful grandchildren, cherished every moment spent with them, their hearts filled with love and gratitude for the blessings that life had bestowed upon them.

Grandparenthood and Lingering Longing

Yet, amidst the happiness, a longing lingered in Harris's heart. With each passing year and every milestone, the distance between him and Naina grew wider. Her memory, however, remained vivid, a constant companion in his thoughts.

He yearned to know what had transpired and caused her parents to break their promise. A secret love for Naina still burned within him, refusing to be extinguished.

The Unforgotten Love

Section 2

Empty Nest, Lingering Echoes

The Quietude of an Empty Nest

The condo, once brimming with the laughter and energy of their growing family, now felt strangely quiet. Rajvir and Ashit, with their own families, had flown out of the nest, leaving Harris and Lavanya to navigate the uncharted waters of an empty nest. The silence over their home starkly contrasted with the cacophony of their previous life.

One evening, as Lavanya prepared dinner, the rhythmic chopping of vegetables punctuated the stillness. Harris sat in the living room, his gaze lost in the flickering flames of the fireplace. The crackling of the wood and the soft glow cast dancing shadows on the walls, amplifying the sense of solitude.

"It's so quiet," Lavanya remarked, setting a plate of steaming *pakoras* on the coffee table.

Harris nodded, a wistful smile playing on his lips. "It's different, isn't it? But it's as well... peaceful."

Lavanya joined him on the sofa, her hand finding his hand. "It is. But I miss the boys."

Harris nodded, his gaze fixed on the family photos adorning the wall. "They're building their own lives now, Lavanya. It's what we wanted for them."

But even as he spoke, a sense of loneliness crept into his heart. He missed his sons, their playful banter, and the shared meals around the dining table.

Music as Solace: A New Pursuit

In an attempt to fill the void, Harris purchased a Casio keyboard. Though the electronic tones were a far cry from the rich melodies of his beloved violin and *'Banjira,'* they offered a creative outlet. He enrolled in an online piano course on Udemy, his fingers stumbling over the keys as he rekindled his passion for music.

In their leisure time, Harris and Lavanya often tuned in to the radio, the nostalgic strains of old Hindi movie songs transporting them back to their youth in India. Lavanya, always quick with a playful remark, would tease Harris whenever a particularly melancholic tune played.

"Ah, another sad song," she'd say with a wink. "Bringing back memories of Naina, are you?"

Harris would blush, his cheeks turning a shade of crimson. "Don't be silly, Lavanya," he'd protest, but a flicker of longing would betray his true feelings.

"Remember this one, Harris?" Lavanya would ask, her eyes twinkling with amusement as an exceptionally sentimental song played. "You used to sing it all the time back in college."

Harris chuckled, a blush creeping into his cheeks. "I wasn't that bad, was I?"

Lavanya playfully nudged him. "You were terrible! But it was endearing."

A Journey Back Home: Lingering Questions

In February 2009, Harris and Lavanya embarked on a trip to India, a pilgrimage to reconnect with their roots and visit Lavanya's parents. Delhi, once their bustling home, now felt like a distant memory. The familiar sights and sounds filled Harris and Lavanya with bittersweet nostalgia, a longing for a past they could never reclaim.

During their visit, Harris made a detour to Jalandhar to see his sister, Vani. As they sat in her cozy living room, sipping *chai*, Harris couldn't shake the feeling that something was missing.

"Vani," he began hesitantly, "have you heard from Naina or her family?"

Vani's expression turned sombre. "Not since your wedding, *bhaiya*. They cut off all ties with us after that."

A pang of sadness pierced Harris's heart. "I can't understand why," he confessed, his voice laced with frustration. "I need to know what happened, what changed their minds."

Vani reached out and squeezed his hand. "I don't have any answers, *bhaiya*. But maybe it's time to let go. It's been so many years."

Harris shook his head, his resolve unwavering. "I can't. Not until I understand."

The Search Begins: A Digital Quest

Back in Toronto, Harris turned to the digital world to find Naina. He spent countless hours scrolling through social media platforms, his fingers flying across the keyboard as he searched for any trace of her. He even tried to locate his old friend, Aman, hoping he might have some information.

But his efforts proved futile. Naina seemed to have vanished without a trace. Had she changed her name? Was she even on social media? The uncertainty gnawed at him, fueling his obsession.

Unaware of the turmoil within her husband, Lavanya noticed his growing preoccupation with the computer.

"Harris," she asked one evening, her voice laced with concern, "is everything alright? You seem distant lately."

Harris forced a smile. "I'm fine, Lavanya. Just a bit busy with work, that's all."

But his words rang hollow, even to his ears. The ghost of Naina constantly reminded him of the denied love lingering in his mind.

Unaware of Harris's feelings for Naina, Lavanya smiled and patted his hand. She trusted her husband, but a nagging worry settled in her heart. She couldn't shake the feeling that this search for Naina was more than a quest for closure. It was a rekindling of a flame that had never indeed died.

The Unforgotten Love

Leo 1953

Chapter 7: Cracks in the Foundation

2011

The Unforgotten Love

Section 1

Haunting Memories and Fractured Bonds

A Successful Career, A Troubled Heart

In 2011, Harris, now 58, was at the peak of his career. His immigration consultancy thrived, and his expertise and dedication earned him the trust and gratitude of clients worldwide. The rhythmic tapping of his keyboard, the soft glow of his computer screen, and the stacks of paperwork on his desk were testaments to his professional success.

Yet, beneath the surface of his accomplishments, a storm raged within him. The memory of Naina, the girl he had loved in silence, refused to fade. Her image, forever etched in his mind, haunted his waking hours and invaded his dreams.

One evening, as he sat alone in his office, the weight of his unspoken love pressed down on him. He reached for his phone, his fingers trembling as he dialled Vani's number in Jalandhar.

"Vani," he pleaded, his voice thick with desperation. Please, help me find Naina. I need to know what happened and why they left."

Vani, on the other end of the line, sighed. "*Bhaiya*, it's been so many years. Why are you still dwelling on the past?"

"I can't let it go, Vani," Harris confessed, his voice cracking with emotion. "I need closure. I need to understand."

Lavanya's Growing Concern

Lavanya observed her husband's growing preoccupation with the past with increasing alarm. His once vibrant spirit seemed to dim, replaced by a distant, haunted look in his eyes. His absent-mindedness and frequent phone calls to Vani raised red flags in her mind.

"Harris," she ventured one evening, her voice laced with concern, "is everything alright? You seem preoccupied lately."

Harris forced a smile, his eyes momentarily leaving the computer screen. "I'm fine, Lavanya. Just a lot on my mind with work."

But Lavanya needed more convincing. She knew him too well. Something else was troubling him, something he wasn't willing to share.

Desperate Measures: The Late-Night Call

One night, as Lavanya lay awake in bed, Harris's restlessness reached a breaking point. He slipped out of bed, the floorboards creaking softly under his feet, and went to the living room. He dialled Mona, Vani's daughter's number, his heart pounding.

"Mona," he whispered urgently, "I need your help."

Mona, startled by the late-night call, groggily answered, "Uncle Harris? Is everything okay?"

"I need you to go to Amritsar," Harris pleaded, his voice thick with desperation. "I need you to find out about Naina, about her family."

Mona hesitated. "Uncle, it's been so many years. Why are you digging up the past?"

"I can't let it go, Mona," Harris's voice cracked with emotion. "I need closure. I need to know why they did what they did."

Mona sighed, her voice filled with concern. "Uncle, please try to forget about Naina. Focus on Aunty Lavanya. She loves you."

Harris's anger flared. "You don't understand, Mona! This isn't just about me. It's about my mother, about the promise they broke."

He hung up the phone, his frustration simmering beneath the surface. He returned to bed, his mind racing with thoughts of Naina, her constant image in his dreams.

Lavanya's Discovery: A Shattered Illusion

Unbeknownst to Harris, Lavanya had been awake, her senses heightened by the hushed conversation. She had heard every word, every plea, every desperate attempt to reconnect with a love lost decades ago.

Tears streamed down her face as she lay in the darkness, her heart aching with a pain she had never imagined. The memory of another woman still consumed the father of her children even after 34 years of marriage.

A Confrontation: The Truth Unveiled

The following day, the tension in the house was palpable. Lavanya confronted Harris, her voice trembling with anger and sadness.

"How could you, Harris?" she demanded, tears streaming down her face. "After all these years, you still haven't forgotten her?"

Harris's heart ached at the sight of his wife's pain. "Lavanya, I..." he stammered, struggling to find the right words.

"Don't 'Lavanya' me!" she retorted. "I've been a good wife to you, a devoted mother to your children. And this is how you repay me? By obsessing over a woman from your past?"

Harris tried to explain, to tell her about the broken promise and the unanswered questions that haunted him. But his words fell on deaf ears, and Lavanya was inconsolable.

The rift between them deepened, their once-harmonious home now filled with the echoes of their unspoken resentments.

A Family Divided: Lavanya's Decision

Desperate to mend the growing divide, Lavanya confided in Rajvir and Geetanjali, her son and daughter-in-law. The revelation shocked and saddened them, momentarily shaking their respect for their father.

They visited Harris and Lavanya one weekend, hoping to mediate the situation. But the tension was too thick, the hurt too deep.

"Papa," Rajvir began tentatively, "we understand that you have unresolved feelings for Naina. But it's been so long. She's probably moved on with her life."

Harris shook his head stubbornly. "I need to know the truth, Rajvir. I need closure."

Lavanya, unable to contain her emotions any longer, burst into tears. "I can't live like this anymore, Harris," she sobbed. "I can't compete with a ghost from your past."

The conversation ended in a stalemate, the tension in the room thick and suffocating. Lavanya, her heart broken and her trust shattered, made a decision that would change their lives forever.

In November 2013, she packed her bags and moved in with Rajvir and Geetanjali, leaving behind the condo and the man she had loved for over three decades. The silence that descended upon their once-happy home was a stark reminder of the unbreakable bonds of the past and the painful reality of a love that refused to die.

The Unforgotten Love

Section 2

A Granddaughter's Quest

The Lingering Silence: Isolation and Longing

The years following Lavanya's departure starkly contrasted with Harris's vibrant life. His immigration consultancy, once a source of pride and purpose, now lay dormant. He dropped his license, the once-familiar legal jargon now a distant echo. Once a sanctuary of family and shared dreams, the condo became a hollow shell, its silence a constant reminder of his fractured marriage.

Even music, once a shared passion with Lavanya, lost its allure. The Casio keyboard gathered dust, its keys untouched. Once filled with the melodies of their shared past, the radio now sat silent, its presence a painful reminder of their broken connection.

Though physically absent, Lavanya remained a constant presence in Harris's thoughts. He yearned for her warmth, laughter, and unwavering support. But her resolve was unwavering. She refused to return to him, her heart wounded by his obsession with Naina.

Saarah: A Bridge Between Two Worlds

Rajvir, Geetanjali, and their daughters, Saarah and Tania, visited Harris every other weekend, a ray of sunshine in his otherwise lonely existence. Saarah, the elder daughter, took it upon herself to bridge the gap between her grandparents.

"*Dadu*," she'd say, her voice filled with concern, "why don't you come and stay with us for a few days? We miss you."

Harris would force a smile, his heart heavy with the knowledge that his home was no longer whole. "I'm alright, *beta*," he'd reply, his voice betraying his loneliness. "You come and visit me instead."

Saarah, wise beyond her years, sensed the underlying sadness in her grandfather's eyes. She often talked to her *Dadi*, Lavanya, trying to understand the reasons behind their separation.

"*Dadi*," she asked one evening, her voice soft, "tell me about Naina Aunty. Why is *Dadu* so fixated on her?"

Lavanya hesitated, her wounds still raw. But Saarah's persistence and genuine concern melted her resolve. She recounted the story, from the initial promise made between the families to the abrupt break-up after Sahil's engagement.

Saarah listened intently, her young mind trying to comprehend the complexities of adult relationships. "It doesn't seem fair,

Dadi," she finally said, her voice filled with empathy. "*Dadu* deserves closure."

A Granddaughter's Bold Plan

An idea sparked in Saarah's mind: a bold plan to help her grandfather find the answers he sought.

"*Dadi*," she proposed, her voice filled with determination, "why don't you accompany *Dadu* to India? He needs to find Naina Aunty and get closure."

Lavanya shook her head, her resolve unwavering. "I can't, Saarah. It's too painful."

Saarah, undeterred, continued, "Then let *Dadu* go alone. I'll go with him. We'll find Naina Aunty and bring back the answers he needs."

Lavanya's eyes widened in surprise. "You'd do that for your *Dadu*?"

Saarah nodded, her resolve firm. "Of course, *Dadi*. I love him, and I want him to be happy."

The Journey Begins: Back to Amritsar

After much deliberation and persuasion, Rajvir and Geetanjali agreed to let Saarah accompany Harris to India. The prospect of visiting her ancestral homeland filled Saarah with excitement, but she also understood the gravity of their mission.

The Unforgotten Love

In September 2017, Harris and Saarah landed at Amritsar International Airport. His hometown's familiar sights and sounds washed over Harris, a bittersweet symphony of nostalgia and regret.

The following day, they hailed a taxi, their destination to the house where Naina and her family once lived. As they approached the familiar street, memories flooded Harris's mind. He could almost hear children's laughter playing in the courtyard, the aroma of Bimal's delicious *'parathas'* wafting through the air.

But as the taxi pulled up in front of the house, a sense of unease settled over him. The house looked different; its once vibrant facade faded and worn. A pang of sadness pierced his heart. So much had changed in the intervening years. Would he find the answers he sought? Or would this journey only lead to more heartbreak?

With a deep breath, Harris stepped out of the taxi, Saarah by his side. The door to the house stood slightly ajar, inviting them into the unknown.

Section 3

The Search for Naina

A Knock on a Door, a Wall of Silence

The old house stood silently under the harsh September sun, its paint peeling and its windows dusty. Saarah, her heart pounding in her chest, pressed the doorbell, its shrill echo momentarily breaking the stillness of the afternoon.

An older man, his face etched with the lines of time, opened the door, peering at them with a curious gaze.

"Can I help you?" he inquired, his voice husky.

"We're looking for Inder's family," Saarah explained, her voice clear and confident. "They used to live on the second floor of this house in 1976."

The man shook his head slowly. "I bought this house in 1985. There were no tenants then."

Harris felt disappointed, a heavyweight settling in his stomach. But Saarah, undeterred, continued their quest, knocking on the neighbours' doors and seeking any information about Naina's family.

"They moved out many years ago," one neighbour recalled, her eyes distant. "They didn't leave any forwarding address."

Dead Ends and Fading Hopes

The next day, Harris and Saarah visited the government girls' college where Naina had studied. The principal, a stern-looking woman with glasses perched on her nose, confirmed that Naina had graduated in 1979.

The principal remarked, "She was a bright student. "She got married shortly before graduation."

The news that Naina was married sent a pang of jealousy through Harris's heart. But it also fueled his determination to find her, to understand why she had chosen another path.

Their search led them to the local Development Authority office, where they hoped to find records of the plot of land Inder had purchased years ago. Surprisingly, the helpful staff retrieved dusty files and traced the land's ownership history.

"It appears Mr. Inder sold the plot in 1984," the clerk informed them, his voice monotonous. "No construction ever took place on it."

Another dead end. Harris's frustration mounted, his hopes dwindling with each passing day.

They visited the girls' school, where Bimal had once been the principal, but they needed help to provide helpful information. A trip to the woollen mill where Inder had worked yielded the same result—he had left in 1984, leaving no forwarding address.

As a last resort, they decided to visit Aman's house, hoping he might know Naina's whereabouts. But to their dismay, they learned that Aman had moved to the UK years ago.

The Crushing Weight of Disappointment

The search had yielded nothing but disappointment. Harris, his spirit broken, retreated into his condo, the silence a stark contrast to the bustling streets of Amritsar he had once known.

He barely left his apartment, eating takeout and microwaved leftovers. The vibrant melodies of his Casio keyboard fell silent, replaced by the sad hum of his thoughts.

Though still residing with Rajvir, Lavanya couldn't ignore the toll Harris's obsession had taken on him. She worried about his health, his isolation, and the growing distance between them.

Rajvir and Geetanjali, worried about Harris's well-being, started visiting him every other weekend. Saarah continued to call her *Dadu*, her cheerful voice a ray of sunshine in his otherwise bleak world.

"*Dadu*," she'd say, her voice filled with love, "when are you coming to visit us again? We miss you."

Harris would force a smile, his heart heavy with the knowledge that he had let his obsession with the past overshadow the present. He had allowed the ghost of Naina to steal his joy, peace, and connection with his family.

Harris's isolation deepened as the days turned into weeks and the weeks into months. The unanswered questions continued to gnaw at him, a constant reminder of the lost love. But amidst the darkness, a flicker of realization began to emerge. It was time to let go, to accept that some questions would remain unanswered, and to focus on the love that surrounded him in the present.

Leo 1953

Chapter 8: Rekindled Connections

2021

The Unforgotten Love

Section 1

An Unexpected Call, a Long-Awaited Encounter

A Voice from the Past

The summer sun of June 2021 bathed Harris's condo in a warm glow, and the gentle hum of the air conditioner was a soothing backdrop to the quiet solitude he had grown accustomed to. The persistent ringing of his phone startled him, the unknown number flashing on the screen. He hesitated, a flicker of curiosity battling his usual aversion to unfamiliar calls.

The ringing stopped, but a few hours later, it resumed. This time, a voicemail notification blinked on the screen. Harris, his curiosity piqued, listened to the message.

"Harsh, it's Aman. I'm in Toronto with my family. It's been ages, buddy. I'd love to catch up. Give me a call when you get this."

Aman's voice, a familiar echo from the past, sent Harris a jolt of excitement. He hadn't heard from his college friend in over thirty years.

"Aman!" Harris exclaimed into the phone as he returned the call. "It's so good to hear from you! Where are you?"

Aman's cheerful voice filled the line. "We're in Toronto for a few days, then heading to Vancouver and Banff. How are you, Harsh? How's *bhabhi*?"

Harris's heart skipped a beat at the mention of his estranged wife. "We're... we're doing okay," he replied, his voice betraying a hint of sadness. "I'll tell you everything when we meet."

They agreed to meet at Rajvir's house the following weekend. Harris hung up the phone, a whirlwind of emotions swirling within him. He longed to reconnect with Aman, but the prospect of seeing him after so many years filled him with excitement and trepidation.

A Surprise for Lavanya

Harris immediately called Saarah, his granddaughter, to share the news. "Saarah, guess what? Aman is in Canada! He's coming to visit us next weekend."

Saarah squealed with delight. "That's amazing, *Dadu*! I can't wait to meet him!"

She had heard countless stories about Aman from her grandfather, their shared adventures in Amritsar etched in her memory.

"I'm going to tell *Dadi* right now!" Saarah exclaimed, her voice bubbling with excitement.

Lavanya's initial reaction was one of disbelief. "Aman? Here? After all these years?"

Saarah nodded enthusiastically. "Yes, *Dadi*! He's coming with his family. *Dadu* is so excited!"

Lavanya's expression softened, but a hint of bitterness lingered in her eyes. "He never bothered to call us all these years," she muttered. "And now he suddenly wants to reconnect?"

Saarah, sensing her grandmother's reluctance, gently coaxed her. "*Dadi*, please. It would mean so much to *Dadu*. And it would be nice for us to meet Aman Uncle and his family."

After much persuasion, Lavanya finally agreed.

A Reunion, A Revelation

The day of the reunion arrived, and Harris, his heart filled with nervous excitement, arrived at Rajvir's house early to help with the preparations. The aroma of Geetanjali's cooking filled the air, a symphony of spices and flavours that promised a delightful feast.

In the afternoon, Aman and his family arrived. Harris's breath caught in his throat as he saw Aman step out of the car, his once youthful face now etched with the lines of time. But his eyes still held the same warmth and mischief that Harris remembered from their college days.

Aman embraced Harris, their laughter echoing through the years. "It's so good to see you, my friend," Aman said, his voice thick with emotion.

He then introduced his wife, daughter and grandson, his gaze lingering on his wife for a moment longer than necessary.

"Harsh," he said, a playful smile tugging at his lips, "I don't think you've met my wife. She is Naina."

The world seemed to tilt on its axis as Harris stared at the woman before him. Although she was older and more mature, her eyes still held the same sparkle, and her smile the same warmth that had captivated him all those years ago.

Naina, too, was taken aback. Her eyes widened in surprise, and a gasp escaped her lips. "Harsh?" she breathed, her voice barely a whisper.

Tania, Rajvir's younger daughter, rushed upstairs to inform *Dadi*. Her excited squeal broke the silence. "*Dadi! Dadi! Dadu's Naina is here!*"

Lavanya's face paled. "What?" she whispered, her voice barely audible.

"Tania, are you joking?" "How can she be here with Aman?" Lavanya said.

Sensing the tension in the air, Aman rushed upstairs to meet Lavanya. "*Bhabhi*," he said, his voice gentle, "come downstairs. There's someone I want you to meet."

Lavanya, her heart pounding in her chest, emerged from her room, her eyes searching for the woman who had haunted her husband's thoughts for so long.

As Lavanya entered the room, her gaze fell upon Naina. The two women stood frozen, their past and present colliding in profound realization.

Aman's gentle voice broke the silence. "*Bhabhi*," he said, addressing Lavanya with respect, "it's been a long time."

Lavanya nodded, her eyes still locked with Naina's. A complex mix of emotions swirled within her - surprise, anger, hurt, and a flicker of curiosity.

The reunion brought back bittersweet memories of a lost love and a broken promise. But it was also a chance for healing, understanding, and perhaps forgiveness.

The Unforgotten Love

Section 2

Unraveling the Tapestry of Time

A Long-Awaited Introduction

As Aman gently guided his wife towards Lavanya, the air crackled with anticipation and awkwardness.

"*Bhabhi*," he said, his voice warm, "I'd like you to meet my wife, Nalini."

Harris's breath hitched in his throat. Nalini? The name felt foreign, yet the face... it was unmistakably her. Naina, the girl who had haunted his dreams for decades, stood before him with a gentle smile.

Lavanya, though taken aback, extended her hand. "It's a pleasure to meet you, Nalini," she said, her voice surprisingly steady.

Once filled with youthful exuberance, Nalini's eyes now held a depth of experience and warmth. "The pleasure is all mine, Lavanya."

Aman then introduced their daughter, Anamika, a vibrant woman with a contagious laugh, and her teenage son, Rupesh, a quiet but observant young man.

The once-silent house now buzzed with conversation and laughter. Rajvir and Geetanjali, their daughters Saarah and Tania clinging to their sides exchanged greetings with Aman's family. The aroma of Geetanjali's cooking filled the air, promising a feast of flavours and shared stories.

Unraveling the Past

As they settled into comfortable chairs, curiosity hung heavy in the air.

"Aman," Harris finally said, his voice a mix of eagerness and apprehension, "how did this happen? When... when did you and Naina...?"

Aman chuckled a hint of nostalgia in his eyes. "It's quite a story, my friend."

He glanced at Nalini, a silent conversation passing between them.

"Before we came to Canada," Aman began, "I called Zara to get your number. Remember Zara? Aarna's friend?"

Harris nodded, the memories flooding back. "Of course, I remember Zara. We met at my wedding."

"Well, after your wedding, I stayed in touch with her," Aman continued. "She's the one who gave me your contact here."

A wave of realization washed over Harris. Zara, the mischievous girl who had once teased him during the *'joota chupai'* ritual at his wedding, had unknowingly played a pivotal role in reuniting him with his past.

A Flashback: Aman and Naina's Story

Aman's voice softened as he delved into the past. "After you married Lavanya, I grew closer to Nalini. We started dating, and her parents, Inder and Bimal, really liked me. They arranged our marriage in 1978."

"My parents loved her," Aman continued. "They thought she was perfect for me. They even changed her name to Nalini for astrological reasons."

Harris's heart ached at the revelation. Nalini. That's why he couldn't find her on social media. The pieces of the puzzle were finally falling into place.

"And then, in 1979, we had Anamika," Aman continued, his gaze filled with paternal pride.

"The unrest in Punjab forced us to leave Amritsar in '84. We moved to London, where I now manage a car dealership, and Nalini teaches at high school."

Anamika smiled warmly at Harris and Lavanya. "It's an honor to finally meet you both. I've heard so much about you."

Her son, Rupesh, a lanky teenager with a mop of curly hair, added shyly, "Hello, Uncle and Aunty."

Life in London: A New Chapter

Aman's story continued, painting a picture of their life in London. He had become a car dealership's general manager while Nalini, the dedicated educator, taught at a high school. Their daughter, Anamika, had grown up and married, and they were now proud grandparents to Rupesh, a bright young man pursuing a degree in computer science.

"Life has been good to us," Aman concluded, his voice filled with contentment. "We've built a happy life in London."

A Tapestry of Emotions

The room fell silent as everyone absorbed the revelations. Lavanya's heart ached for Harris, the pain of his lost love etched on his face. Yet, there was also a sense of relief, a release from unanswered questions.

Nalini, her eyes meeting Harris's across the room, tentatively smiled. "I'm sorry for the pain we caused you, Harsh," she said softly. We never meant to hurt you."

Harris nodded, his smile bittersweet. "I understand, Naina. It was a long time ago."

As the afternoon progressed, the conversation flowed more easily, laughter mingling with shared memories and stories of their lives. Once a source of pain and confusion, the past now served as a bridge, connecting two families and two generations.

Leo 1953

The reunion was a testament to the resilience of the human spirit, the ability to heal and forgive, and the enduring power of love, even in its unspoken form.

The Unforgotten Love

Section 3

Echoes of the Past, Whispers of the Heart

Naina's Truth: Unveiling the Past

All eyes turned to Nalini, a hush falling over the room. It was her turn to unveil the secrets that had shaped their destinies. She took a deep breath, her gaze meeting Harris's across the room.

"After your father passed away, Harsh," she began, her voice soft yet firm, "my parents had reservations about our marriage."

Harris's heart ached. He had always suspected that his father's death had played a role in their separation, but hearing it confirmed it brought a fresh wave of pain.

"They were concerned about our age difference," Nalini continued. "And they also felt that... well, that I was taller than you."

A ripple of surprised laughter passed through the room, breaking the tension momentarily.

"But the main reason," Nalini's voice faltered slightly, "was that they had grown fond of Sahil. They thought he would be a more suitable match for me."

Harris's jaw clenched. He had always known Sahil was the favoured son, the charmer, the one who effortlessly won hearts. But hearing that her parents preferred his younger brother over him stung deeply.

"When Sahil got engaged," Nalini continued, her eyes glistening with unshed tears, "it devastated them." They had been waiting for the right moment to tell your mother about their change of heart, but the news of his engagement shattered their hopes."

She paused, her gaze meeting Harris's once again. "So, they used my studies as an excuse. They told your mother I needed more time to complete my education."

A heavy silence descended upon the room. The truth, once hidden in the shadows of the past, now lay exposed, its raw edges cutting deep.

Geetanjali's Curiosity: Unlocking Hidden Emotions

Geetanjali, Harris's daughter-in-law, couldn't contain her curiosity any longer. "Nalini Aunty," she ventured, her voice gentle, "did you... did you ever want to marry Papa?"

Nalini's eyes softened. "Of course, I did," she admitted, a wistful smile touching her lips. "We had grown up together, shared so many memories. And... I had feelings for him."

She glanced at Aman, a silent understanding passing between them. "Aman and I often talk about Harsh, about his love for me. Every year, on our birthday, I would think of him, wondering where he was, what he was doing."

Harris's heart ached with a bittersweet longing. He had carried Naina's memory in his heart for all these years, and knowing she had felt the same way brought joy and sorrow.

"Did you ever want to meet him again?" Geetanjali pressed further.

Nalini nodded. "In 2002, after Rupesh was born, we visited my parents in Rohtak. Aman and I decided to take a detour to Amritsar. We went to your old house, Harsh, hoping to catch a glimpse of you."

Echoes in an Empty House

The familiar sights and sounds of the city evoked a bittersweet nostalgia, a reminder of the intertwined lives that had once unfolded within its bustling streets. A wave of apprehension washed over him as they stood before the faded blue door.

They knocked on the door, and a young boy, his face framed by tousled hair and curious eyes, answered.

"Hello," Aman greeted him with a warm smile. "We're looking for the family of Vishwas and Simran. They used to live here many years ago."

The boy's brow furrowed in thought. "I'm sorry," he replied, "but this house has changed hands many times. No one here knows who lived here before."

Disappointment flickered across Aman's face. It seemed like another dead end in their quest for answers.

But then, the boy's eyes lit up. "Wait," he said, "I did find the name 'Harsh' carved into a concrete shelf in one of the rooms. Maybe they knew someone named Harsh?"

Hope surged through Aman. "Can we see it?" he asked eagerly.

The boy nodded and led them inside. Now a dimly lit cloth storehouse, the house held a faint echo of the past. Dust motes danced in the air, and the smell of old fabric hung heavy in the atmosphere.

In one of the rooms, they found the shelf, its surface marred by time and neglect. And there, etched into the gray concrete, was the name "Harsh," a tangible link to his childhood.

"It may be his parents," Aman whispered, his voice thick with emotion. "They must have carved it when he was a child."

Nalini's eyes filled with tears. "It's beautiful," she murmured, reaching out to trace the letters.

A wave of regret washed over Harris. His pain had so consumed him that he had failed to see the love that had always surrounded him.

Section 4

Closure and New Beginnings

A Tapestry of Missed Opportunities

The room fell silent, the weight of their shared history hanging heavy. It was a story of love, loss, missed opportunities, and unspoken truths.

Aman, sensing the emotional undercurrent, cleared his throat. "We never meant to hurt you, Harsh," he said sincerely. "Our parents' decisions were their own, but Nalini and I always cherished our memories of you."

Harris nodded, a sense of understanding dawning upon him. "I know, Aman. I don't blame you or Naina. It was just... bad timing."

He turned to Nalini, his eyes filled with sadness and gratitude. "Thank you for telling me the truth, Naina. It means a lot."

Nalini smiled gently. "You're welcome, Harsh. I'm glad we finally had a chance to talk."

The Unexpressed Love: A Flame Rekindled

As the conversation continued, the layers of the past peeled away, revealing the depth of the unspoken love that had once bound Harris and Nalini. In their well-intentioned efforts to secure their children's happiness, their parents had inadvertently extinguished a flame that had burned brightly in their young hearts.

But now, in this unexpected reunion, that flame flickered back to life, casting a warm glow over their shared memories and unspoken desires. The years of separation and silence melted away, replaced by a sense of connection transcending time and circumstance.

As the evening drew close, Harris and Nalini stood on the balcony, gazing at the Toronto skyline. The city lights twinkled in the distance, their cold glow contrasting with the warmth between them.

"I never stopped thinking about you, Naina," Harris confessed, his voice husky with emotion.

Nalini's eyes shimmered with unshed tears. "And I never stopped thinking about you, Harsh."

At that moment, the unspoken words of their youth finally found their voice, echoing through the years and bridging the gap that had separated them for so long.

A Feast of Forgiveness

Harris, his voice thick with emotion, addressed Lavanya. "I'm so sorry for the pain I've caused you, Lavanya. My obsession with Naina... it was selfish and unfair."

Lavanya's eyes, rimmed with tears, met his. "I understand, Harris," she said softly. "But it hurt. It felt like all these years, I wasn't enough."

Harris reached across the table, taking her hand in his. "You are more than enough, Lavanya. You've always been my strength, my partner. I was a fool to let the past cloud my vision."

He turned to Nalini, his gaze filled with remorse. "And Naina... I'm sorry for what my family did. I never stopped caring for you."

Nalini's smile was bittersweet. "There's no need for apologies, Harsh. We were all young, caught in circumstances beyond our control."

A comfortable silence fell over the table, broken only by the clinking of cutlery and the soft murmur of conversation. Harris's thoughts drifted back to his mother, Simran.

"I'm grateful to *Biji* for arranging my marriage to Lavanya," he said, his voice filled with newfound appreciation. "She gave me a gift I didn't fully understand at the time."

He looked at Lavanya, his eyes shining with love and gratitude. "You've stood by me through thick and thin, Lavanya. Without you, I wouldn't be the man I am today."

Lavanya's tears flowed freely now, but they were tears of relief and reconciliation. "I love you, Harris," she whispered. I never want to lose you."

A New Generation's Hope

As the evening progressed, laughter filled the room, the warmth of reunion thawing the chill of past grievances. Nalini, her eyes twinkling, turned to Geetanjali.

"Geetanjali," she said playfully, "what do you think about Rupesh and Saarah? They would make a lovely couple, wouldn't they?"

A chorus of laughter erupted, the suggestion a welcome reminder of the future and the possibility of new beginnings.

Geetanjali smiled. "It's a lovely thought, Nalini Aunty. But let's not repeat the mistakes of the past. We'll let them choose their own paths."

A sense of peace settled over them as the night drew to a close. The past, with its tangled threads and unspoken truths, had finally been laid to rest. The present, filled with the warmth of family and the promise of new connections, beckoned them forward.

Harris and Lavanya, their love rekindled, walked hand-in-hand toward their car, the city lights reflecting in their eyes. The journey had been long and arduous, but they had finally found their way back to each other.

Leo 1953

The Unforgotten Love

Characters

(In alphabetical order)

Character name – Relation to the main character – A brief introduction of the character

Aman (Close friend) - Harsh's close friend from college, a carefree spirit who becomes a confidante and source of support. Later he revealed to be married to Naina.

Aarna (Sister-in-law) - Lavanya's younger sister, a lively and social young woman.

Amar (Brother-in-law) - Vani's husband, a bank manager, chosen for his responsible nature and good character.

Ashit (Son) - Harsh and Lavanya's second son, who follows in his father's footsteps by pursuing a career in finance and eventually takes on a leadership role in Hong Kong.

Baldev (Tenant-formerly) - A tenant in Simran's house, a quiet and unassuming man who marries Kumud's sister, Suman.

Baljit (Sahil's father-in-law) - Kumud and Suman's father, who arranges their marriages to Sahil and Baldev, respectively.

Bimal (Naina's mother) - Naina's mother and Simran's college friend, a school principal who plays a pivotal role in the families' intertwined destinies.

Divya (Daughter-in-law) - Ashit's wife, originally from Delhi, who works in a call center in Toronto and shares his dreams for the future.

Geetanjali (Daughter-in-law) - Rajvir's wife, a kind and intelligent woman who works in IT for a bank.

Harsh/Harris - The protagonist of the story. A dedicated and resilient man who navigates love, loss, and career changes across continents.

Inder (Naina's father) - Naina's father, a lawyer who works for a private company.

Kumud (Sister-in-law) - Sahil's wife, a vibrant young woman from Ludhiana whose family becomes closely connected with Harsh's family.

Lalit (Former Boss) - Vishwas's boss and an IAS officer who offers Harsh a job after his father's passing.

Lavanya (Wife) - Harsh's wife, a kind and supportive woman who stands by him through life's ups and downs.

Laxmiya (Grandmother-in-law) - Simran's mother, who provides guidance and support to her daughter and grandchildren.

Mohin (Father-in-law) - Lavanya's father, who initially hesitates but ultimately approves of Harsh as a suitable match for his daughter.

Maninder (Nephew) - Sahil and Kumud's second son, adding to the growing family network.

Mona (Niece) - Vani's daughter, who initially resists Harsh's request to search for Naina but ultimately plays a role in facilitating the reunion.

Naina/Nalini (Childhood love, Aman's wife) - The girl Harsh falls in love with in his youth, whose family's sudden departure leaves a lasting impact on his life. Later revealed to be married to Aman.

Vani (Sister) - Harsh's younger sister, who marries Amar and remains a close confidante throughout his life.

Pushpa (Sahil's mother-in-law) - Kumud and Suman's mother, who supports her husband in arranging their daughters' marriages.

Rajvir (Son) - Harsh and Lavanya's firstborn son, who pursues a career in finance and marries Geetanjali.

Rakshita (Mother-in-law) - Lavanya's mother, who welcomes Harsh into their family and supports his marriage to her daughter.

Rupesh (Aman's Grandson) - Aman and Naina's grandson, who represents the next generation and the potential for new connections between the families.

Saarah (Granddaughter) - Rajvir and Geetanjali's daughter, who plays a pivotal role in reuniting Harsh with his past and encouraging reconciliation with Lavanya.

Sahil (Brother) - Harsh's younger brother, who marries Kumud and remains a close companion throughout his life.

Simran (Mother) - Harsh's mother, a loving and supportive figure who guides him through the challenges of life. Her friendship with Bimal intertwines the destinies of their families.

Suman (No relation) - Kumud's sister, who marries Baldev and moves out of Simran's house.

Surjit (Former Boss) - Harsh's boss in Jalandhar, who recognizes his legal skills and offers him a new opportunity.

Tanveer (Grandson) - Ashit and Divya's son, adding to the expanding family network.

Tania (Granddaughter) - Rajvir and Geetanjali's second daughter, further expanding the family.

Vishwas (Father) - Harsh's father, a dedicated government officer whose untimely death leaves a profound impact on the family.

Vikram (No relation) - The leader of the employees' union at Harsh's workplace, who offers support and guidance to Harsh after his father's passing.

Yoginder (Nephew) - Sahil and Kumud's first son, adding to the family network.

Zara (No relation) - A close friend of Lavanya's sister, Aarna, who unknowingly plays a role in reuniting Harsh with Aman and Naina by providing Aman with Harsh's contact information.

Leo 1953

The Unforgotten Love

Glossary

(In alphabetical order)

Hindi words – English translation

Baraat - The groom's wedding procession, typically a lively celebration with music, dance, and revelry.

Bhaiya - An affectionate term for an elder brother, often used by younger siblings or close relatives.

Bhabhi - Elder brother's wife.

Bhangra - A lively Punjabi folk dance, often performed during celebrations and weddings.

Chunni - A traditional headscarf or veil worn by women, often given to the bride as a symbol of acceptance into the groom's family.

Chana Dal - Split chickpeas or lentils, often fed to the mare during the Ghud Chadi as a symbol of prosperity.

Dadu - Grandfather (paternal).

Dadi - Grandmother (paternal).

Desi Ghee - Clarified butter, a staple in Indian cooking.

Dhaba - A roadside restaurant or eatery, typically serving Punjabi cuisine.

Didi - Elder sister.

Doli - The decorated car or palanquin in which the bride is transported to her new home after the wedding.

Dupatta - A long scarf or shawl worn by women, often draped over the head or shoulders.

Ghud Chadi - The tradition of the groom riding a mare to the wedding venue.

Haldi - Turmeric, a yellow spice often used in Indian cuisine and traditional rituals, known for its auspicious and medicinal properties.

Halwai - A confectioner or sweet-maker, specializing in traditional Indian sweets and snacks.

Jaimala - The exchange of floral garlands between the bride and groom, signifying their acceptance of each other.

Jalebi - A popular Indian sweet made from deep-fried batter soaked in sugar syrup, known for its intricate spiral shape.

Joota Chupai - A playful tradition where the bride's sisters or friends hide the groom's shoes, demanding a ransom in return.

Kanyadaan - The traditional ceremony where the father of the bride gives away his daughter to the groom, symbolizing his blessings and entrustment.

Kewra - A fragrant floral water extracted from the Pandanus flower, often used in Indian desserts and rituals.

Lehenga - A long, embroidered skirt worn by women, typically paired with a blouse and dupatta, often worn on special occasions like weddings.

Mantras - Sacred verses or hymns chanted during Hindu rituals, believed to invoke divine blessings and protection.

Mehandi - Henna, a natural dye used to create intricate designs on the hands and feet, often applied during weddings and festivals.

Nani - Maternal grandmother.

Pagri - Turban.

Pandit - A Hindu priest or scholar, well-versed in religious rituals and scriptures.

Paratha - A layered flatbread, a staple in North Indian cuisine.

Phera - The ritual of circumambulating the sacred fire during the wedding ceremony, symbolizing the couple's journey together.

Pooja/Puja - A Hindu prayer ritual, often involving offerings, chanting of mantras, and seeking blessings from deities.

Rasam Pagri - A ceremony where a turban is tied on the head of the male heir of the deceased.

Roka - An engagement ceremony in North Indian tradition.

Saab/Sahib - A term of respect added after a man's name.

Sangeet - A pre-wedding celebration filled with music, dance, and merriment, often involving both the bride's and groom's families.

Sehra - A decorative veil or headgear worn by the groom during the wedding ceremony, often covering his face.

Shagun - An auspicious gift or token given during special occasions, often symbolizing blessings and good wishes.

Sitar - A plucked, stringed instrument, prominent in North Indian classical music.

Tilak - A mark made on the forehead, usually with vermilion paste, signifying blessings and good fortune.

Vidaai - The emotional farewell ceremony where the bride leaves her parental home to start a new life with her husband.

Printed in Great Britain
by Amazon